THE
WEREDUCK
CODE

Book 3 of the Wereduck series

Dave Atkinson

NIMBUS
PUBLISHING
— NIMBUS.CA —

Praise for CURE FOR WEREDUCK

Cure for Wereduck is as silly and fun as it is believable: you'll be checking your friends for feathers at every full moon. Dave Atkinson's roll-off-the-tongue dialogue and smooth, vivid action make this novel a page-turner kids will simply enjoy. With cliffhanging scenes in all the right places, I cannot wait for book three!

—*Meghan Marentette, author of* The Stowaways

Fans will be happy to see that this book starts right where *Wereduck* ended. I may be *slightly* older than the target age group, but that didn't stop me from enjoying this fast-paced fun read. *Cure for Wereduck* mixes a generous portion of action and adventure with plenty of humour.

—*Riel Nason, author of 2012 Commonwealth Book Prize–winning* The Town That Drowned

Dave Atkinson's *Cure for Wereduck* is a rollicking good story, with equal measures of mystery, drama, and humour. The wereduck variation of werewolf is a wonderful invention. Readers will love the duck named Wacka in both her duckly and wereduckly forms.

This novel is just plain fun. Read it. You'll see.

—*Deirdre Kessler, children's author and Prince Edward Island poet laureate*

Young readers' praise for WEREDUCK

I rate *Wereduck* 10/10 and will be one of the first to buy the next books.

—*John*

I really enjoyed reading your book! You are an amazing author and I hope that I will become one too.

—*Bonnie*

I'm writing to thank you for coming all this way to our West Royalty Elementary School and telling us about *Wereduck*. I loved it. I read it all. It's AMAZING! Good luck in your new book. I hope it's as good as *Wereduck*. I wasn't into reading too much but when I read your book I loved it so now I'm reading more!

—*Diego*

Copyright © 2019, Dave Atkinson

Nimbus Publishing Limited
3660 Strawberry Hill St, Halifax, NS B3K 5A9
(902) 455-4286 nimbus.ca

Printed and bound in Canada

NB1477

Cover and interior illustration and design: Jenn Embree
Editor: Emily MacKinnon | Proofreader: Penelope Jackson

This is a work of fiction. Names, characters, incidents, and places, including organizations and institutions, are either the product of the author's imagination or are used fictitiously.

Library and Archives Canada Cataloguing in Publication

Title: The wereduck code / Dave Atkinson.
Names: Atkinson, Dave, 1978- author.
Identifiers: Canadiana (print) 20190152486 | Canadiana (ebook) 20190152508 | ISBN 9781771087988 (softcover) | ISBN 9781771088015 (HTML)
Classification: LCC PS8601.T5528 W48 2019 | DDC jC813/.6—dc23

Nimbus Publishing acknowledges the financial support for its publishing activities from the Government of Canada, the Canada Council for the Arts, and from the Province of Nova Scotia. We are pleased to work in partnership with the Province of Nova Scotia to develop and promote our creative industries for the benefit of all Nova Scotians.

To the Wednesday night D&D crew:

Alice, Finley, Jane, Henry, Padraigh,

Seamus, and Stewart.

You slayed the lich.

You saved the world.

You rode a T-Rex named Jeff.

PROLOGUE

TABLOID JOURNALIST/COUNTRY SINGER STILL MISSING

*Investigation into unexplained disappearance
stretches to eighth month*

NEW YORK—POLICE SAY THERE ARE STILL NO NEW
leads in a mysterious missing-person case involving
a reporter at the infamous and journalistically dubi-
ous tabloid newspaper *Really Real News*. Dirk Bragg,
a senior investigative reporter at the paper, failed to
show up to work the day after filing a bizarre story
involving werewolves and a previously unheard of beast
from even the most fantastical fairy tale: a wereduck.
Bragg, whom friends and colleagues variously describe
as a "paranoid conspiracy theorist," a "superstitious
nut job," and an "outright lunatic," hasn't been seen
or heard from since.

"Dirk started acting weird after coming back from a work trip to Canada last November," said Sandra Postcop, managing editor at *Really Real News*. "I'm not going to lie to you—that's saying something. Dirk's kind of an odd bird at the best of times, but those last couple of days? *Hoo boy!* He was acting strange. Kept mumbling about werewolves and trains, and he was rubbing tube after tube of antibacterial hand sanitizer on a scratch on his ankle."

Police are stumped by the case and haven't ruled out any possibility, including foul play. They also say, given what they've learned about Bragg's personality, he may have gone into hiding.

"Yeah, that'd be just like Dirk," acknowledged Postcop. "One time he wrote a story about how taxi drivers could read people's thoughts and how they were planning to use this power to pull off the biggest electronic bank heist in history. After that, he became terrified of every yellow car on the street. He went into hiding for, like, five weeks? I mean, I love the guy, but he can be a bit cuckoo."

In a peculiar twist to an already-peculiar story, the second single from Dirk Bragg's debut album climbed to the top of the country music charts this week. "A Bunch of Bananas (and This Lonely Heart)" is currently the most popular country song in the nation. It replaces another song by Bragg, "My Wheels Belong to the Road (But My Heart Belongs to You)," which held onto the top spot for an impressive 13 weeks. Bragg recorded his debut album, *Tabloid Blues*, in the weeks before he went missing, but hasn't appeared publicly to celebrate its meteoric success. A statement released from his label, B & M Records, says it prays for Bragg's safety and hopes he comes home soon to record another album.

CHAPTER ONE

KATE THUNDERED DOWN THE STAIRS TO THE basement. Her long, brown hair streamed behind her as she leapt over the pile of dirty laundry in front of the washing machine and burst through her bedroom door.

"G'morning, Wacka!" she shouted.

A little mallard glared at Kate through half-closed eyes and resettled herself into a warm corner of her nest.

Kate flipped open her laptop and tapped her finger impatiently as she waited for the chat window to load.

Loading...

Still loading...

A little green light popped up beside John's name. A tiny excited duck fluttered in her stomach. Kate clicked on his name and began to type.

Kate: Oh good!!! Glad I caught you.

A few seconds passed as she waited for his reply.

John: Forgot about the hour time difference between Ontario and New Brunswick, did ya? I'm going to be late on my first day.
Kate: I just wanted to say good luck!
John: I can't believe Mum is actually going through with sending me to school.
Kate: It might be kind of fun! I always wondered what it was like to be a normal kid and go to normal school.

The screen sat idle for a moment.

John: Kate, they don't come any less normal than you.

Kate smiled. He was the same old John, even half a country away.

Kate: Well, they don't come any more MORON than you.
John: BTW, that thing arrived in the mail yesterday.
Kate: That thing?
John: That icky DNA thing.
Kate: Oh, THAT thing! Did you do it?
John: Yeah, it was no big deal. It's just a swab inside your cheek. I sent it back already.
Kate: Oh cool! Mine should be arriving soon too!
John: Yeah. Listen, I really need to go. My actual bus is waiting to take me to actual school.
Kate: Have a good day! Don't make a new best friend.

The screen was quiet for a moment. Kate thought he had logged off, until…

John: Ain't gonna happen, pal. ;)

Kate shut her laptop and leaned back in her chair. She looked around her little basement room. When she'd first moved last summer with her family from their camp in New Brunswick to this little farmhouse in southern Ontario, she'd hated it. Her whole family and John were packed like sardines, but it was the safest place they could be after nearly being exposed to the world by that gross reporter, Dirk Bragg (better known by Kate and John as Dirt Bag).

It turned out to be John's dad, Marcus, who had led Dirt Bag straight to them. Marcus had been so tired of running from the reporter, he was willing to sell out Kate's family to the front pages of *Really Real News* in exchange for his freedom. But when John wasn't willing to betray his new friends, Marcus didn't take it well. He abandoned John in the forest, leaving Kate's family to take care of him.

So much had happened since then. If she hadn't lived through it, she wouldn't have believed it.

For starters, John discovered his mother was actually alive. It was a huge shock, since his dad had told him his entire life she was dead. John, Kate, and their duck friend, Wacka (who was a reverse wereduck— long story) travelled to New Brunswick to meet her. It didn't…go well. John's mum mistook werewolf John for werewolf Marcus, who had stolen John from her. She shot him with a silver bullet. Marcus showed up just in time to save John with something called the Cure for Werewolf. The silver bullet killed the werewolf within John, but he survived. He was now just plain old John.

Which brought them to today. John had moved in with his mother in Moncton. Her full-time job got in the way of his homeschooling, so she decided to enroll him in the local high school. John was far from enthusiastic, but had reluctantly agreed it was for the best.

Kate's stomach rumbled. She yawned and headed back upstairs to the noises and smells of a big family breakfast.

"Your tea's cold," said Grandma Marge as Kate slid into the seat next to her at the table. "A crime against the world's most perfect drink."

Kate smirked as she topped up her half-empty cup from the pot. "Sorry, Grandma. I wanted to catch John before his first day of school."

"Oh, that's right," said her father, Brian, from across the table. "My favourite son is heading to class."

"Hey!" objected Bobby, Kate's twelve-year-old brother. "What am I, chopped liver?"

In the short time he had lived with them, John had endeared himself to Kate and Bobby's parents by getting a job, spending his spare time studying at the library, and generally being a helpful presence around the house.

Brian pushed his chair back. "Why don't you come dry the dishes, and maybe we can renegotiate your place in the pecking order?"

Marge stood up. "He can't. My favourite grandson has already volunteered to help me clean out the loft in the barn."

Bobby scowled. "Is it still volunteering if it wasn't my idea?"

"Semantics," said Marge, pulling on her boots.

Bobby cleared his plate and followed his grandmother to the door.

"And if we finish the barn by this afternoon, you can volunteer to help stack firewood," said Marge. She opened the door for her grandson and flashed him a big smile.

"I sure do seem helpful today," said Bobby.

"That's what's so refreshing about you!" said his grandmother, as the door swung closed behind them.

Kate grinned as she buttered a slice of toast.

"How did you manage to dodge that bullet?" asked her mother from across the table.

"Who do you think she volunteered to chop the firewood in the first place?" replied Kate. "Grandma told me last night I had signed up for *that* job."

Her parents' laughter was interrupted by the slam of the front door. Kate's aunt Bea walked into the kitchen. She was sorting a small pile of mail.

"You almost ready for work, Lisa?" said Bea, not looking up.

"Just need to grab my tool belt, and I'm good to go," said Kate's mother, finishing the dregs in her cup.

Bea flicked through bills and flyers. She paused at a thicker, padded envelope and eyed the address suspiciously. "Mrs. Katherine El Duckminster," she read. She looked at her niece with a raised eyebrow. "You?"

"It came!" exclaimed Kate, jumping from her seat and snatching the envelope.

"What the heck is that all about?" asked Brian as he watched Kate tear open the envelope.

Kate laid the contents on the kitchen counter: a slender plastic tube, a long stick, and a few pages of printed instructions.

"Home DNA kit!" announced Kate, scanning the instructions.

Her parents and aunt stared at her. Her mother broke the silence.

"A...home DNA kit?"

"Yeah!" said Kate, as if the allure of such a product would be obvious to anyone.

"Kate," prodded her father. "*Whyyyy*?"

Kate looked up from the paper into the confused faces of her family.

"I'm testing John's and my DNA," she explained. "I'm trying to figure out the whole 'werewolf' thing on a genetic level. With John suddenly not a werewolf anymore, it gives me a chance to test my theory that there's a protein switch embedded within the so-called 'junk DNA' that remains inactive in the ninety-eighth percentile of the human genome that is assumed to be non-coding!" Her eyes sparkled.

Brian's stare went from Kate to his wife, and back to Kate. "Kate, you know your mother and I love you very much, but...*what*?"

Kate sighed. "I've just been doing a little research about DNA and human genetics," she said. "Haven't you ever been curious about why you live in a werewolf family?"

Brian let out a breath and raised his eyebrows. "I guess," he said with a little shrug.

"Kate, it's impressive that your understanding of science is so...advanced," said Lisa carefully. "But, don't you think it's a bit...dangerous to be sending this kind of information to a company that might find werewolf and wereduck DNA a bit, well, suspicious?"

"No, it's perfect!" said Kate, holding up the paperwork. "Look!" She smoothed the paper on the counter in front of her. "I chose this company really carefully." She pointed at a series of check boxes. "You can choose for them to screen your DNA for a number of factors—genetic markers for disease, that sort of thing—or, you can just leave it all blank and check the last box."

Her finger underlined the last option on the page. It read: *Don't screen for anything, just send me my genetic sequence. Discretion: GUARANTEED.*

"See?" said Kate. "It's perfect."

"I hope so, Katie," said Lisa. "The last thing we want after the year we've had is someone finding out there's a family of werewolves living here."

"Don't worry, Mum. I'll be careful."

Her mother ran her hand down Kate's hair and kissed the top of her head. "I know you will, sweetie."

"You ready?" said Aunt Bea from the front door.

"Right," said Lisa. "Work. Right." She picked up a tool belt draped over a chair.

"Have a good day, Mum," said Kate.

Kate gathered the contents of her envelope and took them downstairs to her bedroom. She dropped everything on her bed, plopped down beside them, and scanned the instructions once more.

"This doesn't look too hard, Wacka," said Kate without looking up. "I just have to scrape a sample from inside my cheek."

She popped open the plastic tube. Inside was what looked like a Q-tip, but about twice the normal size. She opened her mouth and began to rub gently on the flesh just inside her mouth.

"There," she said after a minute. She removed the swab and placed it back in the container. "Now I just package it up and pop it in the mail. Want to come to the mailbox, Wacka?"

The room was quiet.

"Wacka?" said Kate, looking up.

The little mallard lay in her nest. Her eyes were still closed. She wasn't moving. Kate rushed to her side.

"Wacka, what's wrong?"

CHAPTER TWO

JOHN SHIFTED HIS WEIGHT IN HIS CHAIR. IT WAS HIS last class in what was already a long first day.

The actual school part wasn't too bad. He wasn't as far behind in math as he'd worried. His history teacher was likeable. His geography teacher looked like he wanted to be there even less than his students did.

It was the people part of school that didn't make any sense. No one spoke to him in his homeroom. He thought that might be a fluke, so he tried to talk to the kids around him in his first-period class. Two boys responded to his greeting with blank stares. The girl in the desk next to him rolled her eyes and turned to have a discussion with a kid in the next row. He ate his lunch in the cafeteria by himself. He waited out the excruciating final minutes of the lunch hour sitting on the floor in front of his locker.

John glanced at the clock now. In fifty-six minutes, his first day would be over. He could go home and try to forget it.

"All right, all right, all right," said the English teacher. "Settle down. Take your seats."

When the scraping and shuffling of chairs ended, the teacher stood up. "Okay," he said. "Welcome back. I hope your spring break was...fruitful. We're going to start right back up where we left off with Hinton's *The Outsiders*. Now, if you could all turn to page—"

"Sorry, Mr. Scribbage?" said a girl sitting directly to John's left. She had dyed black hair and wore a dark grey hoodie. On the cover of her notebook, she'd doodled the names and logos of several metal bands. "Aren't you forgetting something?"

The teacher peered over his glasses. "Yes, Jolene? What did I forget?"

She pointed at John, who was seated next to her. "New guy," she said, not even turning her head look at him.

John slouched in his chair, wishing all those eyes weren't suddenly staring at him.

"Right," replied Mr. Scribbage. "New guy, indeed. Thank you, Jolene. Class," he said, addressing the rest of the students, "as Jolene so astutely points out, we're joined for the last half of the term by a *new guy*. I trust you'll all make John feel welcome. He's just transferred in, and he was homeschooled up to this point. Welcome, John."

John smiled weakly. "Thanks," he muttered.

The students murmured for a moment as Mr. Scribbage grabbed a paperback from his desk and leafed through its pages.

"Homeschooled?" whispered Jolene. "So, like, were you locked in your house for the last fifteen years? Are you terrified of human contact?"

John tapped the eraser of his pencil on his desk and stared forward. "Something like that," he said.

"Okay!" announced Mr. Scribbage, pushing his glasses back up the bridge of his nose. "We're going to be reading aloud, starting at chapter six. Justin, if you wouldn't mind—"

Mr. Scribbage was interrupted again, this time by a sharp knock on the door. He crossed the front of the classroom and pulled the door open. A pair of burly police officers stood in the hallway. After a short, whispered conversation, Mr. Scribbage turned back to the class.

"John?" he said. "These officers would like a word with you."

John looked around the class. Yet again, every eye was on him. This time, their look of dull apathy was replaced with genuine shock.

John slowly stood up.

"Bring your books," said one of the police officers. "You won't be coming back."

"Ooooooooooh," said several kids in the class.

Jolene leaned over as John gathered his belongings. "Police on your first day?" she whispered. "*You'll* be a fun addition to this boring school, New Guy."

John clutched his books to his chest like a shield as he walked past the rows of staring students. Mr. Scribbage watched him leave with his eyebrows raised halfway up his forehead. The door closed behind John, leaving him alone in the hallway with the two police officers.

"Come with us," said one briskly. They turned and walked through the halls, finally entering the main office. John had already been here this morning, registering for his first day of school. One of the police officers greeted the secretary at the front desk.

"Is this him?" he asked.

She looked straight at John. Her lips were thin. She nodded.

"Thank you," said the other officer. He pointed toward a door marked with *Vice Principal Schultz* on the nameplate. "Can we use this office?"

"Yes," she said. "Dr. Schultz is out this afternoon."

The first officer held the door as John entered. The room was decorated with cheap wood panelling and an ugly brown shag carpet. The carpet in front of the desk had been trampled flat by years of students coming in to face the music.

"Chair," said the second officer, pointing to the uncomfortable-looking wooden chair set in front of the vice-principal's desk. John sat.

Both officers leaned against the desk, uncomfortably close to John. They both crossed their arms. It was a well-rehearsed routine to make someone feel small. It was working perfectly.

"I'm Constable Dufour," said the first officer. He nodded his partner. "This is Constable Anderson."

"Nice to meet you," said John.

"Okay, let's get down to it," said Anderson. He had a thick moustache and a chiselled brush cut. "You've got some explaining to do."

"I don't understand," said John.

"Well, you're not the only one," said Dufour. He was as burly as his partner but clean-shaven and slightly balding. "Why don't you start by explaining how a child listed as missing for the past fifteen years registered for classes this morning at Moncton High?" he said. "I'm awfully curious."

CHAPTER THREE

"I DON'T KNOW WHAT TO TELL YOU, KATIE," SAID Marge, crouching beside Wacka's nest. She gently stroked the little duck's back. "I can't see anything wrong with her."

Wacka stirred, readjusting herself in her nest. Her head and bill rested on her chest. Her eyes were closed.

Wacka was no ordinary duck. They had first met back on Kate's thirteenth birthday, when Kate learned to quack at the full moon. While the rest of her family transformed into wolves once a month, Kate became what she'd always wanted to be: a duck. On the night of her first transformation, she'd met Wacka in a nearby lake. The two had been inseparable ever since, especially since Wacka was bitten by a werewolf.

The bite of werewolf usually turns the victim into a werewolf. Wacka, being a plain old female mallard, became something very different. On the night of the full moon, she became a girl.

"But she's never like this, Grandma," said Kate, frowning. "She's got to be sick or hurt or something. She's barely moved since this morning."

"Look," said Marge, standing up. "I'm not a vet, but I've given her a good look. She's got no cuts or bruises. She doesn't have a fever. Her breathing is fine. None of her joints seem to be bothering her."

"She barely touched her food this morning," insisted Kate. She sat on the ground next to Wacka's nest and laid her hand on the duck's back.

"It's true," began Marge. "The only thing I can think of, Kate, is that Wacka is, well, Wacka is…."

"What? What is she? Is it bad? *Is she dying*?"

"No, no. Nothing like that. I just think Wacka's got a case of the blues."

Kate stared at her. "The *blues*?"

Marge nodded.

"You're saying my duck is sad."

Marge gave her shoulders a little shrug. "I think so."

"Wacka can't be sad!" said Kate. "She loves it here! She has her own little nest! Dad dug her that little pond in the yard. Everything is great!"

"I'm not saying you aren't taking good care of her," said Kate's grandmother. "I'm just saying I think something is bothering her. And you, as her friend, need to figure out what that is." Marge leaned in to give Wacka a kiss on the bill. "Take care, little one. I hope you're feeling better."

Wacka opened her eyes halfway. "Wacka," she quacked.

Marge put a hand on Kate's shoulder. "You'll figure it out," she said. The door shut behind her as she left the room.

Kate sat beside the nest, absently petting Wacka. The duck breathed a heavy sigh.

"Is that it, Wacka?" asked Kate. "Are you sad?"

Wacka looked Kate in the eyes. She closed them again and nodded. "Wacka."

She and Kate had long ago established a code: one quack for yes, two for no.

"Oh, sweetie. I'm sorry," said Kate. She traced the side of the duck's face with her finger. "Do you know why you're sad? Is something bothering you?"

Wacka shook her head and gave two quacks.

"Just sort of blue?" suggested Kate.

"Wacka," said Wacka, closing her eyes again.

Kate stood up and paced the room. A ball of stress rolled around in her stomach. Wacka was Kate's responsibility, and she had let her down. Worse than that, she was one of Kate's two best friends in the whole world, and she hadn't even noticed she was sad until it had come to this.

Kate turned to face her friend. "Wacka," she announced in a clear, confident voice. "You better finish up that breakfast. You're going to need all the energy you can cram in. I am going to give you the best day of your little ducky life."

CHAPTER FOUR

MARGE CROSSED THE BACKYARD AND WALKED under the pair of maple trees. At the back corner of the lot stood a little wooden barn that had long ago stopped housing livestock. For a generation or two, it had become the spot where the occupants of the farm tossed their junk when they didn't know what else to do with it.

Marge entered the barn and looked around. The main floor was swept clean to the concrete. Marge was proud of that. She'd worked by herself for a few weeks clearing out rusty farm machinery and broken tools.

"Grandma, are you going to help up here or what?" came Bobby's voice from above.

The upper loft, thought Marge, was a different story.

"Keep your shirt on," she answered, climbing the rungs of the rough wood ladder that led to the old hayloft. "I'm coming."

"Grandma, this is going to take forever," whined Bobby when his grandmother appeared. He picked up an old electric kettle from a cluttered workbench. The handle came loose from the rest of the kettle in his hands. He tossed it in the growing pile of junk in the middle of the loft.

Marge sighed. "It seems like it now, but you've done a lot in a short while," she said, surveying his work.

It was true. Despite his whining, Bobby had put a good dent in the sorting and tossing to reclaim the space.

"Does that mean I can go?"

"Ha," she said. "Not likely.

Bobby deflated and reached for another piece of junk on the workbench.

"Oh, hey," he said. "How's Wacka?"

"She'll be fine," said Marge, picking up an old VCR and turning it over to decide whether it was junk or salvage. "Nothing serious. Kate'll figure it out. That little duck's just got a case of the blues."

Bobby made a face. "The blues?" he asked.

"Yeah, you know," said Marge. She tossed the VCR on the junk pile and held an imaginary guitar in her hands. "*Well since my baby migrated*," she sang, closing her eyes. "*I found a new nest to dwell. It's at the cold end of the pond. I've got the ducky blue-oooooooos!*"

Bobby narrowed his eyes. "You're weird," he said.

"I think that's where *you* get it," said Marge cheerfully. She picked up a stack of tin buckets. Every single one was rusted right through the bottom. She tossed them in the junk pile.

Bobby turned back to the workbench. Something silver caught his eye, peeking out from under a pile of dusty canvas.

"Hey, Grandma," he said, moving the canvas so he could grab the item. "Look, I found you a microphone. Now you can take your blues act on the—*whoa*!"

Bobby grasped an old-fashioned microphone sitting on a tabletop stand. A thick cable connected it to an electronic device that looked like it was straight out of a 1950s spy comic.

"*Cool*," said Bobby.

"What'd you find?" asked his grandmother, looking over his shoulder.

"I don't know!" he exclaimed. "Help me clean it off."

Marge lifted a corner of the canvas and peeked under. "Oh my."

"What is it?"

"Help me get this drop cloth off, and I'll show you," said Marge. "Someone obviously wanted to keep the dust off."

Bobby grabbed a corner. They carefully slid the canvas cover from a pile of equipment. The microphone was attached to a metal box covered in dials, switches, and analogue displays.

"Whoa!" said Bobby. "It's like a whole radio station!"

Bobby followed a length of insulated wire and found an old set of over-ear headphones at the end. Another cable ran up the wall and through a hole drilled in the ceiling.

"*Coooool*," he repeated.

Marge examined the main box. "'RF-Master 2000,'" she read. "Hmmm...."

"What is it, Grandma?"

"I think it's an old ham radio," she said.

"What's ham radio?" he asked. "Like, radio for pigs?"

"No," she said, smiling. "Ham radio is what people call amateur radio. It's a set of frequencies set aside for anyone to use. Anyone who has the technology and know-how can broadcast themselves."

"Like a CB radio?" asked Bobby. "In a semi-truck?"

"Kind of," said Marge. "But more powerful. Ham operators can talk to each other from the other side of the world. I think they can even talk to people on the International Space Station."

"No way!" exclaimed Bobby. He flipped a switch back and forth on the base of the microphone. "Think it still works?"

"I don't know," said Marge, eyeing the main box. "All the cables seem fine. The one going through the ceiling must be attached to the antenna on the roof of the barn. We may need to change the old vacuum tubes, and the whole thing needs a good cleaning."

"Let's do it!"

"Tell you what," she said. "If we can get the rest of the loft cleaned by lunch, we'll give it a go this afternoon."

"Deal!"

CHAPTER FIVE

JOHN PUT HIS HEAD DOWN AND WALKED OUT OF the vice-principal's office. The secretary watched him leave. The cops had let him go, but it had been awkward. They had so many questions about where he'd been all these years. They were especially interested in what had become of his dad. John was relieved to be able to answer honestly: he had no idea.

He had less than ten metres to walk from the school's main office to the front doors, but it might as well have been ten kilometres. A crowd of kids had gathered at the doors, hoping to catch a glimpse of what exactly was going on with the police. He recognized a few from his English class. He plowed toward the exit and tried to imagine what muscle he had to flex to turn himself invisible.

He emerged from the main doors into the afternoon sun. He hooked his thumbs around the straps on his backpack and started toward home.

When his feet touched sidewalk, he sighed. He was no longer at school. He could leave this stupid day behind.

"New Guy, wait up," said a girl's voice.

John winced.

Jolene, the dark-haired girl from class, sidled up beside him, her hands dug deep in the pockets of her hoodie. "You had a heck of a first day."

"Yeah, well," he said, not knowing exactly how to handle this. "I guess."

"What'd the police want, New Guy?" she asked, falling into step beside him.

John let out a breath. "Nothing."

"Nothing?" she repeated. "Riiiight."

"It was nothing," he said. "They just wanted to ask me questions about...stuff."

"Oh, okay," she said, nodding. "That's not suspicious at all. Totally normal. Yup."

John grumbled.

"Listen, New Guy, while you were gone, Scribbage assigned us as partners for the next independent study. We need to read a piece of *modern fiction*," she said, looking disdainful at the words, "and write a report on it. Mr. Scribbage's idea of modern fiction is stories about werewolves or sparkly vampires. So naturally, I chose sparkly vampires."

John stopped walking. "You don't like werewolves?"

Jolene rolled her eyes. "Please," she said. "Talk about the lamest horror myth ever. I'd rather die than read a dumb story about werewolves."

John raised his eyebrows. "I always thought werewolves were kind of...mysterious."

Jolene scoffed. "*Ah-wooooooooooooo waaaah* I want my mommy!'" she mocked. "Bunch of lonely babies howling in the woods, if you ask me."

John considered this. "Huh," he said finally.

Jolene swung her backpack off her shoulders and dug into it. "So, here's the sparkly vampires book. We need to read it by next week and give a presentation on Friday." She handed him a copy of a tattered, well-read paperback.

"Okay, thanks," he said, taking the book.

"Gotta go," said Jolene, looking at her phone. "Somewhere I need to be. See ya later, New Guy."

John watched her take a few steps.

"Hey," he called after her.

She stopped.

"My name is John."

She swivelled away. "Whatever, New Guy."

John continued walking, passing the book from hand to hand before slipping it into the front pocket of his jacket.

He wasn't quite ready to be home yet. He knew his mum would be full of questions about his first day. He knew she'd understand. She'd probably even make him a grilled-cheese sandwich and a bowl of tomato soup—the secret ingredients to feeling better—but he just needed a few more minutes to himself.

He stopped at a small wooded park a few blocks from home and headed for a bench tucked into a stand of trees near the back. He pulled out the book and tried to read. After scanning the first sentence three times, the words just weren't sticking in his brain.

He'd tried to be okay with all the new things in his life. It was nice living with his mum and getting to know her. But it was a different life than the one he'd known on the road with his dad for fifteen years. Now he had a bed, a room, and a house. He had a home. It was wonderful. It was just...different.

He'd barely gotten used to the idea that he'd have to go to school, and suddenly there he was, sitting in class. But instead of a first day of navigating the lunch line, apathetic teachers, and weird kids (although it was those things, too) it was cops, questions, and the dull stare of suspicious teens.

John rubbed his eyes and tried that first sentence one more time.

"So, how was your first day?" said a voice behind him.

John jumped.

"Dad!" he gasped.

Marcus grinned at him from the shadows of the trees.

John scowled. "You shouldn't be here," he whispered.

"I didn't want to miss my boy's first day of school," said Marcus.

"No, seriously," said John urgently. "Dad, the cops are freaking out because I suddenly showed up out of nowhere."

"Hmm," said Marcus. He thought for a moment. "I guess we should have expected that. Kid missing for fifteen years suddenly shows up at school."

"And I thought the worst part would be finding my classes," said John.

"What's the big deal?" said Marcus. "They can't exactly hold you responsible. I'm sure this will pass."

"Maybe," said John. "But it's not me the police care about. It's *you* they want, Dad. They're calling you a kidnapper."

CHAPTER SIX

WACKA'S EYES BULGED. SHE PEEKED FROM THE basket mounted on the handlebars of Kate's bike as they sped along the trail.

"Hoooooold on, Wacka!" shouted Kate.

The old bike rattled as Kate careened over the bumps and ridges of the dirt path. She stood on the pedals as she coaxed the bike up a sharp rise and hit the brakes when she reached the top.

It was a clear and beautiful day. The sky was blue. The sun was warm.

"Look at that, Wacka," she said, looking down over the crest of the hill. "What do you think?"

The ground in front of them dropped down a rocky embankment to an almost perfectly rectangular lake. It was like nothing Wacka had ever seen before.

"Aunt Bea says this was a gravel quarry, years and years ago," said Kate, looking around. "But they dug too deep and hit groundwater. It started to pour in from below. *Poof.* Instant lake. Bea says no one knows exactly how deep it is. Cool, huh?"

Wacka looked around. The steep banks sheltered the surface of the water from the wind, but a bit of breeze had snuck through to cause a tiny ripple along one side of the lake.

"Want to go for a swim?" asked Kate.

Wacka perked up. She looked at Kate to see if she was serious. Peering over the side of her basket, she gave an enthusiastic quack.

"All right," said Kate with a sparkle in her eye. She tightened the strap on her helmet and adjusted her grip on the bike's handles. "Better hold on to something."

"Wacka?" quacked Wacka, swivelling back to look at Kate.

"Let's go!" shouted Kate.

"Waaaaaack!" quacked Wacka as the bike started to roll down the hill.

Kate barely had to push the pedals before gravity took over. The bank was steeper than she anticipated. Within a few seconds, they were rolling at a dangerous speed. Rocks and bushes whooshed past so quickly they blurred in their peripheral vision.

The bike shook and wobbled as Kate struggled to keep control. Kate was starting to have second thoughts as they bounced down the hill.

"Waaaaack!" quacked Wacka, spotting a fork in the trail ahead. The left path would take them straight into a dense bramble of scrubby trees and bushes. The right path swerved toward a cliff edge several metres above the lake.

"Hooooooold on, Wacka!" shouted Kate, choosing the right fork.

"Waaaaaaack!"

Time slowed as bike, duck, and girl launched off the edge of the cliff. Wacka flapped her wings to free herself from the bike's basket. Kate flew over the handlebars in a mad dive to hit the water as far from the bike as she could.

SPLASH!

Rings of ripples radiated from the spot where Kate hit the water. Wacka landed neatly and paddled to the spot where her friend went under.

"Wacka?" quacked the duck. She ducked her head under the water.

Kate's grinning face whooshed toward Wacka's as she swam to the surface, her hair swirling in the water.

Kate splashed to the surface. She beamed at her friend.

"I guess we'll have to walk home, huh?" said Kate.

Wacka closed her eyes and made the most curious sound. If Kate had to guess, she would say the little duck was laughing.

"Oh, Wacka," said Kate, beaming from ear to ear. "Are you still sad?"

Wacka paddled closer and leaned her cheek against Kate's. It was as nice a hug as Kate had ever received.

"Wacka wacka."

CHAPTER SEVEN

BOBBY CROUCHED BESIDE THE WORKBENCH TO watch his grandmother work. She had removed the outer box of the radio unit and was now using a can of compressed air to carefully clean the dust from the circuitry inside.

"Now let's replace these tubes," she said, popping what looked to Bobby like a funny light bulb from a tiny socket. She held it up to the light to see the mechanism inside. "Yeah, these have seen some wear." She set it aside and picked up a small white box. "Luckily, whoever used it kept spares around."

"This is so freaking cool, Grandma," said Bobby, as she carefully popped the glass tube into place.

She gave the tube a little nudge to make sure it was snug. "I haven't changed one of those in forty years," she said to herself.

"So, is that it? Can we plug it in and turn it on?" asked Bobby.

"That's it," said Marge, replacing the cover on the box. "Though I can't promise it'll work. Anything beyond changing the tubes and taping up a few frayed wires is beyond me. But we can give it a try."

Bobby grabbed the plug and inserted it in the wall socket. Marge flipped the power switch on the front of the unit.

"We've got to let the tubes warm up first," said Marge. "Should just take a minute."

"I didn't know you knew so much about ancient technology."

Marge stared at him. "Later, I can show you how we can arrange giant stones in a circle to communicate with aliens."

"*Coooool*," said Bobby.

Marge sighed.

"That ought to do it," she said after a moment. "Let's crank 'er up and see if she still goes."

Marge picked up the old headphones. "You take one side," she said. "I'll take the other."

Bobby pressed his ear against the small speaker and watched as his grandmother turned a knob marked "Gain." The sound from the earphone was terrible: harsh crackles and fuzzy static.

"Sorry," said Marge, yanking the headphone from her ear. "That's just a dusty switch."

She removed the knob cover and gave the socket a quick blast from her air can. "That ought to do it."

They put the headphones back to their ears, and Marge tried again. This time, as she turned up the gain, Bobby heard light static and squeals, and then... the faint sound of a man's voice.

"It works, Grandma! It works!"

"It does!" she said with a smile. "Now *shhh*."

Marge turned a second dial, this one marked "Frequency." She'd barely touched it when the squeals became quieter and the man's voice became clearer.

"*...oito, quatro, cinco, cinco, dez, nove, oito....*"

"What the heck is that?" asked Bobby.

"Numbers," said his grandmother. "I think it's... Spanish? Or Portuguese."

"Someone went to all the trouble to broadcast themselves to the whole world and they're just saying numbers?" said Bobby. "Can we find another channel?"

"Sure," said Marge, reaching for the frequency knob.

The static and squeals returned, along with snippets of indistinguishable words and voices from weaker signals. Finally...

"*...sechs, sieben, acht, vier, zwei, drei, dreizehn....*"

"Huh," said Marge quietly. "That's interesting."

"What? What's interesting?"

"That's someone counting in German."

"What the *heck*, Grandma?" said Bobby. "I thought this was going to be cool, not Numbers Time at the United Nations."

Marge shrugged. "Sorry," she said, taking off her headphone. She stood up. "I've got to go help your dad with supper. Why don't you see if you can find someone talking about something other than numbers?"

"Yeah, maybe someone will be reciting the alphabet," said Bobby with a pout.

"Just worry about these two knobs," said Marge, pointing. "This one is gain. It's basically your volume.

This one is frequency. Turn that slowly to tune into other stations and other people talking."

"Counting," corrected Bobby. "Other people *counting*."

Marge ruffled his hair and climbed back down the ladder. "See you at supper."

"See you," said Bobby, putting the old headphones over his ears.

Bobby turned up the gain. The man was still rattling off numbers in German. "Das is weirdo," said Bobby to himself. He slowly twisted the frequency knob.

Most of what he found was difficult to make out or too weak to understand. He didn't speak Mandarin, but he was pretty sure one station was a man counting in that language.

"What is wrong with you people?" muttered Bobby.

After cycling through nearly the entire frequency spectrum, he came across a channel unlike any of the others. No static. No squealing. Just a low electronic hum.

"Weird," said Bobby.

He reached for the dial and jumped when the hum began to change. Ever so slowly, the pitch became higher. It climbed until it reached a frequency so high Bobby had to rip the headphones off. He held them at arm's length for a few seconds before tentatively bringing them back to his ears.

The hum was gone. It had been replaced by a voice that had been manipulated to sound like a robot.

"That should make sure none of the *freaks* are listening," said the voice. "You're listening to D-Net. We are your first and last authority on all things werewolf, were*duck*, and the continuing search for the only man brave enough to speak truth to power: a man so dangerous to the status quo, the status quo stole him from us. I'm talking about Dirk Bragg."

Bobby yanked the headphones from his ears. "Holy crud," he whispered into the empty barn.

CHAPTER EIGHT

JOHN STOOD AT THE FRONT DOOR OF A LARGE white house. A pair of black stone lions guarded either side of the entrance. A well-coifed hedge ran around the property. The grounds were so well cared for John guessed there must be a full-time gardener on staff. The entire place reeked of money.

It was not the kind of house John would have thought Jolene lived in.

John reached out to ring the doorbell. A moment later, a woman in her forties opened the door. Her hair was so blonde it was almost white. But not nearly as white as her gleaming smile, which seemed permanently etched on her face.

"Yes?" said the woman. Her smile said, "Welcome," but her eyes said, "Who the heck are *you*?"

"Oh, hi," said John, as politely as he could. "I was wondering if Jolene was home?"

"Jolene?" said the woman through strained eyes. "Oh, you must be Jason, her little homework friend." She looked him up and down.

"John, actually."

"Come right in, Jason," she said, stepping aside. "Or do you prefer that people call you Jay?"

John walked through the door and into a grand foyer. The floor was marble, as was the staircase sweeping to the second floor.

"I usually prefer 'John,'" he said, turning around to take in his surroundings. His mum's entire house could fit inside this room. "You have a lovely home."

"Aren't you nice," she said absently. "Jolene is in the basement playing with her computers," she said. "You can go right on down."

John followed Jolene's mother's instructions to find the basement. He walked through a living room with a fireplace so large you could park a small car inside it. In the kitchen, he found a pair of cooks wearing white jackets and chef hats.

"Basement?" asked John.

One of them pointed to a door beside the walk-in pantry.

"Thanks."

John could see why Jolene would prefer spending time in the basement. The walls were unpainted drywall. The ducts of the house's heating system were exposed on the ceiling. A pool table stood in one corner. Other than the enormity, it could have been the basement of any house.

Jolene was nowhere to be seen. There was a single door leading to another room. John knocked gently.

"I thought I told you I was busy, *Mother*," said Jolene.

John opened the door a crack. The room behind it was dark. "Um," he said. "It's me. John. I came for our...homework thing?"

"Oh. New Guy," said Jolene. "It's you."

She flicked on a lamp. Jolene sat at a desk covered with three giant monitors. Above them were several stacks of metal utility shelves, each displaying an impressive and confusing amount of equipment.

"Close your mouth, New Guy. You look like you've never seen a computer before," said Jolene, turning in her chair to face him.

"Well, I have, but, uh," stammered John. "Not one like this. I guess."

Jolene leaned back. "Huh," she said. She stared at him.

THUNK.

"Ugh," said a male voice.

"Oh," said John with a bit of a start. "I didn't realize you were with somebody."

A burly teenaged boy a few years older than John emerged from behind the rack of computer gear.

Jolene rolled her eyes. "Dude, did you bonk your head *again*?" said Jolene.

The boy nodded, rubbing a spot on his forehead.

"You gotta be careful. Did you fix the server?"

The boy nodded again.

"Good," said Jolene. "That lag is unacceptable from a year-old piece of hardware. It wasn't a storage issue, was it?"

The boy shook his head and held up computer cable, pointing to a frayed bit near the plug at the end.

"Ah, a bad connection," said Jolene. "I guess that explains why the lag was intermittent. Nice work."

The boy nodded and turned back to the console.

"Uh," said John.

"Oh," said Jolene, suddenly remembering John was in the room. "New Guy, this is Thunk. Thunk, this is New Guy."

"Nice to meet you," said John. He offered his hand.

Thunk ignored the handshake and nodded. He retreated back behind the rack of gear.

Jolene smiled. "My brother," she explained.

"Can he...," began John.

"Talk?" said Jolene. "Oh yeah. He just doesn't like to. He's happier building all this stuff than doing just about anything else."

"Cool," said John, nodding.

Jolene turned back to her computer and continued typing as if John weren't there. The silence was awkward.

"Your mum, uh, seems nice," John said finally. "But she seems to think my name is Jason."

Jolene didn't look up. "Honestly, she probably thinks *my* name is Jason." She continued typing. "Hold on, I just have to close a couple conversations."

Jolene deftly typed and clicked, moving her attention from screen to screen. It seemed to John that she must have been speaking with more than dozen people or groups, though she was not using any chat or message program he recognized. All of the windows seemed to display primitive text boxes—the kind preferred by those who would rather write their own program than use a free app from some giant corporation.

Jolene closed a final window on her desktop and looked up. "Okay. Good. What's up?"

"Well," said John, digging into his bag. He drew out the copy of the vampire book they were supposed to report on for English class. "This."

"Right," she said. "Did you read it?"

John grabbed a chair and rolled it toward Jolene. "Yeah," he said, pulling out a notebook and a pen. "And I took some notes we may want to use for our report. Vampires are a weird theme in literature. We could trace their emergence through Gothic fiction in the eighteenth century and talk about how our attitudes toward them have changed, especially the odd shift in the late 1990s. It's really weird how we were totally afraid of them and what they represented—immortal youth, beauty, lust—for, like, hundreds of years, and then, all of a sudden, they're the good guys, right? So if we were to—"

"Yeah, yeah," said Jolene dismissively. She turned back to her computer and pulled up a new text file. "That's all great, but I already finished our report."

She pressed a button, and the printer on a nearby table began to hum. Jolene jumped up, grabbed the stack of papers, and gave half to John.

"You're...done?" he said, staring at the still-warm papers in his hands.

"Duh, New Guy," she said, sitting back into her chair. "You catch on quick."

John read the title out loud. "'Sparkly Vampires: Not as Horrible as Stupid Werewolves.'"

"Like it?" she asked. She tilted her head to one side as she admired the page. "I thought the title had a certain poetry to it."

John scanned the typed pages in his hands. "Almost everything in this report is about werewolves and why you hate them."

"Yup," she said with a grin.

"I guess I'm…confused?"

"But, New Guy," Jolene said, "werewolves are super dumb. Wait. Do you actually *like* werewolves?"

John proceeded delicately. "I don't really have feelings one way or the other about werewolves," he said. "I'm sure some of them are, y'know, nicer than others, but this is supposed to be a report on a vampire book."

"Totally," said Jolene, nodding her head. "It's a report about how vampires aren't anywhere near as lame as werewolves."

John grimaced. "But—"

"Sounds like someone has a soft spot for werewolves," said Jolene. "Tell me, New Guy, what is it you love most about werewolves? Is it their pathetic cries for help in the darkness, or how they represent the fear of the wildness hiding inside each of us?"

John blinked. "What," he began, "are you talking about? We're writing. A report. About a vampire book."

Jolene turned back to her computer and started typing. "I should have specified to Mr. Scribbage that I didn't want to be partnered with a werewolf lover. I'll just have to talk to him Monday about—"

"JOLEEEEEEEENE!" screeched a voice from upstairs. "Jolene! Get up here!"

Jolene cringed. "That's my mum," she said. "Come on."

John followed her up to the kitchen. Her mother's unnatural smile was still plastered on her face.

"The internet thingy in my room is doing that *thing* again," she said to her daughter. She crossed her arms. "Fix it."

Jolene sighed. "Did you try resetting the router?"

"Did I what the what?" said her mother sharply. "Just fix it."

John followed the pair back to the main entrance and up the grand staircase. They walked down a series of hallways and ended just outside the double doors of the master bedroom. Jolene's mum was making snide comments the entire time about how unreliable internet "thingies" are. She also threw in some not-so-subtle remarks about Jolene's helpfulness, or lack thereof.

"I'm sure Jason is very adept at helping *his* mother when her thingies need fixing," she said. "Maybe he fixes them so they don't need fixing again," she added.

"Yeah, *Jason* sounds like a real peach," muttered Jolene.

John took a step back as Jolene and her mum entered the bedroom. "I'll, um, just wait out here while you work on that…thingy," said John.

"No problem, Jason," said Jolene. "Just don't wander off. You might get lost."

John stood in the hallway, cringing at the continued back-and-forth bickering from the bedroom. It seemed like this was a constant state for the two of them. This clearly wasn't a new fight. This was one they'd been having for a long time, and they were just picking up where they left off.

John had had fights with his mum and dad before, but just now it felt like he'd never considered how well he actually got along with both of them.

He didn't intend to start wandering, but he wanted to get out of earshot of their argument. He walked a short way up the hallway and reached a T-shaped intersection. He whistled. Jolene wasn't kidding. This house was huge. It wasn't difficult to imagine getting lost. He made a mental map and turned right.

Just up the hall, a door on the left was slightly open. Plastered to the door was a Black Sabbath poster. It also had a hand-lettered sign that read: *Mum, Keep Out. (That means you, Mum.)*

This was clearly Jolene's room.

He peeked through the crack. What he saw intrigued him, so he "accidentally" bumped the door with an elbow. It swung inward. He let out a gasp.

The room was immaculate. Everything in this room had its place, and almost all of it was a tribute to all things werewolf.

Posters of werewolves. Sketches that showed people transitioning to werewolves. Images of the full moon. Articles cut out from fantasy magazines and tabloid newspapers about the existence of werewolves. Figurines of tiny wolves and wolf-men lined a shelf. John's eyes darted from artifact to artifact. Stacked neatly on the desk in the corner was what looked like dozens of copies of *Really Real News*.

"Enjoying the view, New Guy?" said Jolene from behind.

John jumped. "Oh! I'm...I was just—"

49

Jolene reached past him and pulled the door closed. "Anyone ever tell you it's rude to snoop?"

"I'm really sorry, but...," John stammered. "Werewolves? I thought you hated—"

Jolene's eyes narrowed. She was angry.

"I think it's time for you to leave," she said.

CHAPTER NINE

"OKAY, LET ME REPEAT THIS," SAID THE WAITRESS. "This is a very specific order."

"Sure," said Kate. She was seated at a table on the patio of a restaurant overlooking Lake Erie. She adjusted her sunglasses and ball cap. The sun was just a few degrees above the horizon. She really couldn't have timed this any better.

The waitress looked at her notepad. "One sandwich made with two slices of rye bread, toasted. A layer of smoked turkey, sliced thin. A layer of black forest ham, sliced thick. Cheddar cheese. Swiss cheese. Bacon. Lettuce. Tomato. Onion—"

"Wacka!"

The waitress started.

"Sorry," said Kate, reaching over to touch the pet carrier rested on the chair beside her. "You okay, Wacka?"

"Wacka wacka!" Two quacks for no.

"Oh, right," said Kate. She turned to the waitress. "*Red* onions," she said.

"Excuse me?"

"Can the sandwich have red onions?" asked Kate.

The waitress looked from Kate to the pet carrier.

"Sure," she said, making a note on her pad. "*Red* onions. Mayonnaise. And mustard. That everything?"

"Wacka!"

"Sounds perfect," said Kate with a smile.

"And nothing for the duck?" asked the waitress.

"Nope," said Kate. "She's fine."

"Okay then," said the waitress. She flipped her notebook shut. "That will just be a few minutes."

"Thanks!"

Kate waited a moment for the waitress to disappear back into the restaurant. She leaned forward to whisper to Wacka.

"If this doesn't cheer you up, Wacka, nothing will," said Kate. "This sandwich is going to be legendary. People will sing folk songs about this sandwich."

Wacka gave a quack. It was supposed to sound enthusiastic, but Kate knew better. Her campaign to lift the duck's spirits wasn't going well. Wacka perked up for a few days after their swim at the old quarry, but she had since slumped back into her sadness. Kate woke up every day with a new plan to perk up her friend. This latest plan had to work. It just had to.

Kate looked back to the horizon. The sun was just about to set.

"Okay, Wacka," said Kate. "Let's do this. You ready?"

"Wacka."

"Perfect," Kate replied, standing up.

Kate grabbed the pet carrier and walked into the restaurant. The waitress looked up from behind the counter.

"Your sandwich will be ready in just a—I don't think you're allowed to have pets in here," she said, eyeing the pet carrier.

"Sorry!" said Kate. "I'm just going to grab her some water from the bathroom!"

The waitress looked anxious. "Okay," she said, "but make sure you take it right back outside."

"Promise!" said Kate.

Kate walked into the bathroom and locked the door behind her. She set the carrier on the counter beside the sink and opened it.

"There you go, sweetie," she said. "I know you hate it in there."

Wacka waddled out.

"You remember the plan?" said Kate, removing her ball cap and sunglasses. She set them on the counter.

"Wacka."

"Great! Now we just have to wait for the—"

Kate stopped short, interrupted by a familiar sound.

"*Whoooooooooo?*" called a low voice. It seemed to come from everywhere at once. "*Whooooooooo?*"

She first heard it at sunset on the evening of the first full moon after she turned thirteen. Before then, her parents had described the sound as the "call of the moon." They said it was the moon howling, calling all werewolves to become their alternate selves.

It was only when Kate really listened that she realized it wasn't howling. It was asking her *who* she was and *who* she wanted to be.

And she had quacked in response.

"There it is," said Kate. "Good luck, Wacka."

Kate quacked. As soon as the sound escaped her lips, she could feel herself begin to change. Goose pimples broke out all over her body as she began to shrink. Her shoulders drew farther behind her as her arms flopped awkwardly at her side, before folding neatly on her freshly feathered back.

It was all over in a matter of seconds. Where Kate had stood just a moment before lay a pile of wriggling clothes. Something was struggling to pull itself through the neck hole of the T-shirt.

A pair of hands gently picked up the shirt, unfolding the crumpled layers to reveal a brown mallard duck. Kate stared up into the eyes of her saviour—a teenaged girl.

"WACKA'S GOT YOU, KATIE," said Wacka.

Wacka had undergone the same transformation as Kate in perfect reverse. Ever since being bitten by a werewolf herself, she'd become what Kate referred to as a "reverse wereduck." Every night on the full moon, she transformed into a girl—exactly opposite Kate's transformation into a duck.

"WACKA SO COLD, KATIE!" said Wacka with a voice that was (always) about two notches too loud. She shivered and wrapped her arms around her bare skin. "HOOMAN SKIN IS COLDER THAN DUCK FEATHERS!"

"Quack," replied Kate, hopping from Wacka's arms.

She flapped from the ground to the bathroom counter and waddled into the pet carrier, quacking again at Wacka to move her along.

"OH, RIGHT," said Wacka. "CLOTHES. WACKA FORGOT ABOUT CLOTHES."

Wacka sorted through the pile Kate had left on the ground and got dressed. She was relieved to find Kate had chosen slip-on shoes. Even with human fingers, Wacka found tying laces almost impossible.

Wacka looked at herself in the mirror. She pulled her fingers through her hair to untangle a few obvious knots.

"THERE," she said. "WACKA LOOKS LIKE REGULAR HOOMAN."

Kate quacked from her carrier.

"WHAT'S WRONG, KATIE?"

Kate quacked again.

"THIS IS MUCH HARDER WHEN YOU CAN'T SAY WORDS."

Kate pointed with her bill at the sunglasses and ball cap.

"RIGHT," said Wacka. "HAT. GLASSES. WAITRESS WILL THINK WACKA IS KATIE."

She put on the glasses and hat and looked back at the mirror. She considered her reflection for a moment.

"WACKA DOESN'T THINK SHE LOOKS LIKE KATIE, EVEN WITH HER DIGUISE," said Wacka. "A HAT ISN'T A DISGUISE, KATIE. IT'S JUST A HAT."

Kate sighed. She'd explained this many times earlier when they went over the plan. Kate was a teenaged girl with long, brown hair. Wacka was a teenaged girl with long, brown hair. No, they didn't look exactly alike. But Kate had faith in something she'd learned about human beings: they're so wrapped up thinking about themselves they just don't pay that close attention to others.

There was just no way to explain all this when she was a duck. So Kate closed her eyes and tried to look as confident as she could.

"Quack," she quacked.

Wacka looked alarmed.

"AND WACKA WOULD NEVER QUACK LIKE THAT," said Wacka. "WACKA SAYS 'WACKA,' NOT 'QUACK.'"

Kate sighed again.

"Wacka," she quacked.

Wacka scrunched her face. "NOT 'wack-ah,'" she said. "'WACK-ah.' YOU HAVE TO SAY THE 'WACK' LOUDER THAN THE 'AH.'"

Kate glared at her friend through half-shut ducky eyelids.

"Sandwich up," said a voice from the kitchen.

The waitress looked from the sandwich on the counter to the bathroom door. That girl was taking an awfully long time. Surely it didn't take *this* long to get a drink of water for her duck. She really wasn't supposed to be inside with that thing anyway.

Just as she was considering knocking on the door, the door swung open.

"I GOT MY PET DUCK A DRINK," the girl said loudly, stepping out.

Cheryl took a step back as the girl held the pet carrier in the air.

"THIS IS MY PET DUCK," she said. "SHE WAS THIRSTY."

"Okay," said Cheryl. "Nice ducky. Now, can you please take her outside? She's not supposed to be in the restaurant. I could get in big trouble."

"OKAY, I WILL TAKE HER OUTSIDE," said Wacka.

She lowered the pet carrier and started walking.

"Hey, Cheryl," said a voice. "Check this out!"

Wacka stopped and turned around. A man had emerged from the kitchen. He was tossing fruit in the air in a funny way that Wacka hadn't seen before. He was keeping two apples and a banana in the air in a way that seemed to Wacka almost magical.

"Oh, Jimmy!" said Cheryl. "I haven't seen you juggle in a long time. You're getting better."

"You think?" said Jimmy. He blushed as he tossed the fruit in the air.

Wacka was transfixed. She couldn't stop watching this man throw fruit.

"Okay, ready?" he said. "I've only done this once before. One...two...*three*!"

With all three pieces of fruit in the air, Jimmy spun around. If it had worked, it would have been spectacular, but his timing was off by a fraction of a second.

"Whoop!" he yelped as the banana slipped. He tried to grab it before it hit the floor, but was just able to get a corner of it. He was so busy with the banana he bobbled one of the apples. It spiralled out of control, heading straight toward the waitress.

"Cheryl—duck!"

"NO!" yelled Wacka, as Cheryl dodged the piece of flying fruit. "NO! YOU'RE WRONG!"

Cheryl straightened and looked at Wacka. Jimmy dropped his banana and the remaining apple.

"NO, NOT DUCK!" said Wacka, panting heavily. "GIRL. NORMAL GIRL. I AM NOT A DUCK."

Cheryl and Jimmy looked at each other.

"Hey, relax," said Jimmy. "I was just telling my friend to duck out of the way or she'd be hit by the apple."

Wacka's chest heaved.

"I JUST," she began. "I AM A NORMAL GIRL. I AM HERE TO EAT MY SANDWICH WITH MY PET DUCK, WHO IS A REGULAR DUCK."

"Okay," said Cheryl, raising her hands to assure Wacka. "It's okay. Regular girl. Regular duck."

"REGULAR," said Wacka.

"Why don't you go eat your sandwich?" said Cheryl.

Wacka opened her mouth to answer. She closed it again. She didn't know if this was one of those questions humans ask but don't really want you to answer.

"OKAY," she said.

She turned on her heel and pushed open the patio door.

Wacka was usually a fast eater. On full-moon nights, it wasn't unusual for her to clear through most of the chips in the cupboard. She revelled in eating human food when she was a girl.

Kate watched as Wacka slowly ate her sandwich. Wacka looked tired. She looked sad.

"Quack quack," quacked Kate.

Wacka looked up.

"IT'S A VERY GOOD SANDWICH, KATIE," she said. "THANK YOU. RED ONIONS ARE WACKA'S FAVOURITE."

Kate ached inside. Yet another attempt to cheer up her friend had failed. She didn't know what to do.

Kate quacked twice again. But when her bill closed the second time, the sound of quacking continued—first one quack, then a few more. Kate and Wacka looked up.

Flying a few hundred feet above the patio was a small flock of ducks. They flew in a V pointed north. It was beautiful. The early evening air was crisp and cool. The sun had set a few minutes earlier, but the western sky was still painted red and orange and gold. The ducks flying overhead would soon be touching down for the night.

"KATIE," said Wacka. She unlatched the pet carrier and picked up her friend. She pointed at the ducks in the sky. "THEY'RE GOING HOME. THEY'RE FLYING TO THEIR HOME."

The ducks were now directly overhead, flying fast and free. One arm of their V was slightly longer than the other. A few stragglers at the back of the flock struggled to keep up, but they moved as a group with great speed, all intent on their final destination.

"KATIE, THEY HAVE BEEN AWAY FROM HOME FOR SO LONG," said Wacka, her eyes welling up as she tracked the ducks across the sky. "WACKA

HAS BEEN AWAY FROM HOME, TOO. WACKA WANTS TO—" she stopped herself, remembering the rules of English Kate had been teaching her. "I WANT TO GO HOME, KATIE. I NEED TO GO HOME."

Kate looked into her friend's face. Wacka's home was far away, in New Brunswick. Kate and her family had brought the little injured duck with them when they moved here at the end of last summer. Kate had never stopped to think they'd taken her from her home.

Wacka looked down into Kate's eyes. "CAN I GO HOME?"

Kate didn't know how she could make this happen, but she knew she had to do it.

"Quack," she said.

CHAPTER TEN

A GREY MOUSE SCURRIED ALONG THE TWISTING tunnel of last summer's grass. A bit of dusky sunlight lit the path ahead—a spot where the tunnel opened and would leave him exposed. He stopped to smell the air. It was damp and sweet. Evening was coming. The mouse could already see a big full moon hanging low in the sky. He shuddered. A full moon is dangerous when you're low on the food chain. It's like a floodlight for the benefit of every fox and owl in the forest. The mouse scurried on, confident in the safe source of food he'd recently found, far from the eyes of predators.

The mouse approached the foundation of an old wooden building. A cedar shingle hung loose near the bottom, leaving just enough space for him to squeeze through. He crept through the shadows behind an old bureau before boldly marching out into the flickering candlelight of the room. He'd been here enough times to know there was no danger.

A wind-up radio sat on a nearby table. Reception was terrible, but through the static came a country song:

"So baby, come away with me.
My reporter's sensibilities
detect a strong attraction
and some supernatural action
between me and you-oooooo!
I got the ta-ba-loid bluuuuuues!
I got the ta-bloid blues."

As the fiddles and steel guitar began to fade, the disc jockey's voice broke through the static. "That's 'Tabloid Blues,' by Dirk Bragg. That song is number one on the country charts for the sixth week in a row. If only its mysterious singer were around to appreciate its success. What do you think? Is Bragg hiding? Is he *dead?* Did he hit his head and get amnesia?" The DJ laughed. "Your guess is as good as mine. You're listening to 96.3 FM, home of today's best country. I'm—"

A hand reached out and snapped off the radio. The owner of the hand leaned back in his chair and ran his fingers through his long, grizzled hair and beard.

"Amnesia," he said to himself. "That's a new one."

He craned his neck to look out one of the cabin's tiny windows. The light was fading. The sun would set soon. He sighed.

As the man sat lost in thought, the mouse scurried up the leg of the table. It took a bit of acrobatic climbing to pull himself over the edge, but he made it. He squeaked.

The man started.

"Oh," he said softly. "It's you."

The mouse squeaked again.

"Well, let's see what we have for you tonight."

He extended his palm, and the mouse climbed on, unafraid and quite comfortable with this routine. The man carried the mouse to a row of cupboards at the far end of the cabin.

"I'm afraid we haven't much," he said, yanking open a cupboard to find it bare. "I'm awfully sorry, little buddy. I haven't had a lot of luck in the last couple of days." He opened the next cupboard and found a half-empty jar of…something. "You don't like sauerkraut, do you?"

He held the mouse to the jar to let him get a good sniff. The mouse hid back in his hand.

"Hmmm, maybe you're right," he said, placing the jar back in the cupboard. "It's a little old. Say, what about…."

He opened the next cupboard, knowing full well what was in it. It was a little black, and it was a bit mushy on the one end, but it was still good.

"You like banana, don't you?"

The mouse squeaked.

"Sure you do," said the man, walking back to his seat and setting the mouse on the table. "I don't have much, my little friend," he said as he peeled, "but what I have, I'm happy to share."

He pinched the tip of the banana and offered it to the mouse, who grabbed the food with his front paws and began to nibble.

"Eat up. It's my last one, but I'll go out hunting again tomorrow. Thursday is garbage day, and I know a couple of houses that usually have great stuff."

He took a bite of ripe banana and thought about the life of hiding and foraging he'd made for himself here in the woods. All in all, it wasn't so bad. He didn't really miss the daily grind of the big city. Despite his empty cupboards, most of his days were enjoyable. He'd almost say he was happy.

Almost.

He looked out the window again. The sun was low in the sky.

"It's time," he said to the mouse. He shoved the last bit of banana into his mouth and scooped up his little friend. "Let's get you home."

He walked out the cabin door and toward the woods. He stopped to crouch at the base of a tree. He placed the mouse in the long grass growing around its roots.

"There you go, bud," he said. "Stay safe in there for the rest of the night, okay? I'll try to have some more food for you tomorrow."

The mouse scurried away.

The man stood up and looked to the west. A sliver of sun remained on the horizon. It was almost time. He shuddered and plunged into the forest.

He hated the full moon almost as much as he hated what he had become. He could never show his face in public again. Not ever. He had become something terrible. A freak.

He could feel the creature inside him growing stronger, willing itself to break free. He wished he could stop it, but he couldn't.

He entered a familiar clearing in the middle of the forest. He climbed to a rocky high point on the north slope, just below a big maple tree. It was the place his curse had begun. The place he'd first seen humans become…something hideous. The place he now found himself irresistibly drawn.

The man turned west to see the last bit of sun slip below the horizon. He let out a long breath and turned east where the moon hung fat and full above the trees.

"Whoooooooo?" called a familiar voice. The sound of it seemed to come from everywhere at the same time.

"Who, indeed," said Dirk Bragg, senior investigative reporter for *Really Real News,* and mysterious country singer whose songs were ripping up the charts. "I'm a disgusting, awful, freakish werewolf."

Dirk threw back his head and let out a howl that drew on every bit of angst and pain within him. As the sound echoed around the clearing, he began to change into a giant grey wolf.

CHAPTER ELEVEN

"I'M TELLING YOU: IT'S A BAD IDEA," SAID BRIAN.

"And I'm telling *you*: it will be perfectly safe," said Marge. Her arms were crossed.

"Marge, I know you have the best of intentions here, but we left New Brunswick for a reason," said Brian. He paced the kitchen in front of his mother-in-law. "Dirt Bag—or Dirk Bragg, or whatever we're calling him these days—knows where our old camp is. That's reason enough to never go back."

Kate stood in the doorway between the kitchen and the living room, holding Wacka in her arms and stroking her soft back. Kate had been biting her tongue for most of the conversation. Her grandmother had taken immediately to Kate's suggestion of a trip back to their camp in New Brunswick so Wacka could spend the summer in her native home.

"But he's, like, missing," injected Kate at the mention of Dirk Bragg. "The newspapers say he's been gone for, like, nine months or something."

"You hear that, Brian?" said Marge. "We're safe. He's gone."

"Like, *gone* gone?" said Brian.

"Gone," said Marge firmly.

"That's not what D-Net says," piped up Bobby from a seat at the table.

Everyone turned to face him.

"Sorry, what?" said Brian.

"D-Net says he's still alive but has gone into hiding," said Bobby. "Dirt Bag is out there, and he's going to come back and reveal the truth about—" he looked nervous "—a whole lot of things."

A long silence fell over the room.

"What...the heck...are you talking about?" asked Kate.

"It's what D-Net said!" exclaimed Bobby.

"And what on earth is D-Net?" asked his grandmother.

Bobby blushed. "It's the Dirk-Network," he said. "It's an anonymous collective investigating the whereabouts of the 'only man brave enough to speak truth to power.'"

Kate looked to her astonished father, then to her grandmother, and then back at her brother. "Have you gone insane?"

"It's what they said!" shouted Bobby.

"Bobby, Bobby. It's okay, buddy," soothed Brian. "We're just a little confused. Where did you hear of this D-Net thing?"

"It's on the ham radio," said Bobby. "They use a different frequency every day to broadcast the latest news about Dirk."

"There's news about Dirt Bag?" asked Kate.

"Well, not usually," admitted Bobby. "Usually it's just more theories about where he is and what he might be up to. But every once in a while they have someone who thinks they saw him or something. He's coming back, though. And when he does, a lot of people are going to be in for a big shock."

Brian gave his head a little shake. "This conversation took an odd turn," he said. "What exactly are we going to be in shock about?"

"He's going to reveal the truth!" shouted Bobby. "He's gone underground because he needs to complete his investigations. When he returns to the public eye, all will be revealed!"

"Are you, um, forgetting that what this guy wants to reveal is us?" asked Kate.

Bobby paused for a moment. "Oh yeah," he said. "But, like, there's OTHER stuff, too."

"What kind of other stuff?"

Bobby's eyes narrowed. "Conspiracies," he whispered.

Everyone stared at him.

"Look," said Bobby, "I'm twelve-and-a-half years old. I've still got, like, half a year before I become a werewolf. I gotta have something cool in my life."

Kate sighed. "Can we get back to the actual conversation please?"

"I think maybe we need to monitor Bobby's ham radio use a little closer, but yes," said Marge, her eyes darting back and forth between her grandkids. "I still think it'd be safe to go back to the camp."

Brian raised a finger to say something.

"Oh, stop it, Brian," said Marge. "I'm not suggesting we ALL go. I'm saying I'll take Bobby and Kate and Wacka. Just for the summer. This place is getting crowded with all of us anyway."

Wacka stirred in Kate's arms.

"Doesn't Wacka get a say in all of this?" said Kate. "We're talking about her home!"

"Wacka!" quacked Wacka. She fluttered from Kate's arms and waddled toward a dumbfounded Brian. The little duck leaned all her weight into his ankle. She looked up into his eyes.

"Wacka," she said firmly. "Wacka wacka."

Brian's face flushed red. Kate could see he was starting to crack. She crossed her fingers behind her back.

"No fair using those big ducky eyes," he said.

"Brian," said Marge. "I promise, at the first sign of trouble, we'll leave."

"Well," began Brian, "I suppose...."

Kate cheered.

Bobby leapt to his feet. "Yes!" he yelled. "We're going home!"

Wacka quacked and flew circles around the kitchen, eventually landing into Kate's arms. "You're going home, Wacka!" she said, bouncing her friend up and down.

"Wacka," said Wacka.

"Oh, my gosh!" Kate squealed, placing Wacka on the kitchen counter and starting to dance. Wacka followed suit, bobbing her head up and down.

"Girl, we have so much to do before we leave!" said Kate, executing a spin.

"Wacka," quacked Wacka, closing her eyes and giving her rear end a shake.

"We have to tell John. He's going to freak," said Kate, giving Wacka the double-point with a pair of finger guns.

"Wacka," said Wacka happily, shaking her butt one more time for good measure.

"And we have to pack!" said Kate, throwing an imaginary lasso around her friend and pulling her in.

"Wacka."

"And we have to—"

The kitchen phone rang.

"Oh, dang," said Kate.

She grooved over to it and grabbed the receiver. "Hello?" she said, still pulsing to an imaginary beat.

"Hello," said a woman. "I'm looking for a Katherine El Duckminster."

"Sorry, I think you have the wrong—wait, did you say Duckminster?"

Kate stopped dancing.

"Yes," said the woman. "A Mrs. Katherine El Duckminster?"

Kate cleared her throat. "Well then," she said. "This is she. You can call me Kate."

"Well, Kate," began the woman. "My name is Dr. Beck. I work at HappyGene Incorporated. First I want to thank you for your business, and I want to assure you that your privacy is guaranteed with us."

"Okaaaay," said Kate. "I didn't realize the test included a phone consultation."

"Oh, it doesn't," said Dr. Beck. "Not usually. It's just...I've never spoken with a real wereduck before."

CHAPTER TWELVE

KATE STOOD IN THE LOBBY OF THE RESEARCH complex. A sign on the wall listed all the various labs and offices in the building. She looked up HappyGene Incorporated. It was on the fourth floor.

"Okay," said Kate to herself. "No problem. You can do this."

She walked to the elevator. Her finger hovered over the call button.

She sighed. "No, no, no," she said, speed walking back to the front door. "Maybe you can't do this."

She paused with a hand on the door. "But maybe you *should* do this."

She walked back to the index. Sure enough, HappyGene Incorporated was still on the fourth floor.

Kate did a quick lap of the lobby and plopped on a bench by the door. This was way harder than she had thought. She'd spoken briefly on the phone with

Dr. Beck at HappyGene. She was really nice. It's hard to make that kind of impression over the phone, but she even seemed kind. And trustworthy.

Dr. Beck had invited her to her lab in Windsor, less than an hour's drive from Aunt Bea's farmhouse. After a lot of talking with her parents, they'd agreed to drive her there. She'd convinced them the risk was worth it.

Just now, as she stood in the lobby, she wasn't so sure. As soon as Kate walked into that lab, she'd be inviting another person into her family's secret. Her mum and dad had drilled the importance of that secret remaining a secret into her every day of her life. It's why she grew up far from prying eyes.

But she'd shared her secret this year, too. She smiled as she thought about John and Wacka. Wasn't she a better person, a happier person, for trusting them?

She walked back to the elevator door and pressed the call button. The doors opened a moment later.

"You can do this," said Kate to herself as she stepped on the elevator.

"I knew you could," said a security guy from behind his magazine as the elevator door closed behind Kate.

Kate stared at row upon row of test tubes in the laboratory. On the counter sat a giant white microscope. In the corner, a complicated-looking machine hummed quietly as liquid oozed through a series of tubes and hoses.

"You have such cool stuff," said Kate with wide eyes.

Dr. Beck smiled. "Some of it does more than just look cool."

Kate peered into a cupboard filled with empty glassware. She picked up a test tube and held it up to her eye. "So cool," she said. She pointed to the humming machine in the corner. "Is this the DNA sequencer?"

"That's it," said Dr. Beck.

"Wow," said Kate. She examined the monitor next to the machine. It displayed an array of coloured boxes and numbers that were always shifting and moving around the screen. "I wish I knew what this stuff meant."

"You're interested in science?" asked Dr. Beck.

"Oh, definitely," said Kate. "I mean, I've read a bunch of textbooks and internet articles about proteins and DNA and genes and stuff. I thought I knew a lot, but all this equipment makes me feel like a huge dummy."

Dr. Beck laughed. "If you're reading about DNA for fun at age fourteen, I hardly think you're a dummy," she said. "You certainly knew enough to suspect that there was something peculiar about you and your family at a genetic level."

Kate sat on a stool beside the sequencer. "And was I right?"

Dr. Beck's eyes gleamed. She nodded.

"Yes!" exclaimed Kate, pumping her fist. She then remembered her parents' warning. "Wait," she said. "You aren't going to, like, write about us in science journals and tell all your scientist friends, are you?"

"Oh, my goodness, no," Dr. Beck assured her. "No, I would never do that. Your privacy is the most important thing. And I mean that. I would hate for the rest of the world to know about real werewolves." She blinked. "Or wereducks, as it were. I'm just so glad I finally found you."

"Found me? Were you looking for werewolves?"

Dr. Beck nodded. "It's why I became a scientist in the first place."

"Are *you* a werewolf?"

"No," said Dr. Beck. "But my grampy was. He married a non-werewolf, and none of their kids became werewolves. He kind of hoped it might skip a generation, but no."

She looked sad for a moment before brightening.

"I set up this business so I could, hopefully, find some more werewolves. Then I can maybe figure out what it is that makes them werewolves," she said. "I have basically unlimited access to random samples of DNA, which is perfect. But I've been looking for werewolves for so long I was beginning to think my grampy was the last one, until your sample came in. And wow, what a sample. That's why I invited you here."

"Okay," said Kate. "But how did you know what to look for?"

Dr. Beck smiled. "I have a sample of my grampy's DNA. And because I've sequenced my own DNA, I know what it looks like when those genes have been switched off."

"What do you mean 'switched off?'"

Dr. Beck sat down in front of the sequencer and tapped a few keys. "This is the really cool thing," she said. "You're going to love it. Pull up a stool."

Kate dragged a lab stool beside Dr. Beck.

"Okay, this," said Dr. Beck, "is normal human DNA."

The screen displayed an image of a long chain of coloured dots held together by short, straight lines. The chain seemed to swirl as it went toward the top.

"It looks like a screw or something," said Kate.

"Exactly," said Dr. Beck. "This is the double helix. It's the complex structure of molecules that make a human a human, or a worm a worm, or a—"

"Wereduck a wereduck," interrupted Kate.

"Precisely," said Dr. Beck. "I'm way over-simplifying here, but DNA is made up of genes. As humans evolve, we're always adding new genes, which define new traits. But the funny thing about DNA is we don't ever toss out the old genes—even if we no longer use them. We just switch them off. So a gene that would have been super useful to our ancestors millions of years ago but isn't useful now isn't totally gone. It's just turned off."

"Junk DNA," whispered Kate.

"You really do know your stuff," said Dr. Beck, looking impressed. "So, whole sections of the double helix are what we call 'dormant.' We don't use them. And some of them have been with us so long, they belong to animals that aren't even human."

She tapped a few more keys on the sequencer and brought up another image.

"*This* is werewolf DNA," said Dr. Beck. "I got this from my grampy. It took me a long time to figure out what was different from regular DNA. I'd almost given up. But then one night, I was working late. I didn't real-ize it was the full moon night, but as soon as the sun went down…ka-chunk."

"Ka-chunk?" repeated Kate.

"It looked like someone had flipped a switch on grampy's DNA sample, because suddenly a whole bunch of his active DNA went dormant, and a whole section of dormant DNA became active. And the genes that became active were wolf genes."

Kate's eyes widened. "How?"

"Because of this," said Dr. Beck. She hit a key on the sequencer, and a single spot on the double helix began to flash.

"What is it?"

"It's a switch," said Dr. Beck. "A switch made out of a single protein molecule. When it's pointed one way, it turns on the human genes and turns off the wolf genes. When it's pointed the other way, it turns off the human genes and turns on the wolf genes. It's like a toggle."

"Holy cow," said Kate.

"So that's how I look for werewolves," said Dr. Beck. "When people like you send in a sample for me to test, after I do all the other stuff, I check for that protein. And yours is the first one I've ever seen. And wouldn't you know—you weren't a werewolf at all. I can't believe you're a wereduck."

"How did you know that part?"

"Because I could see which genes the switch activated," Dr. Beck replied. "They sure as heck weren't wolf genes. I could see they were fowl, and for a while, I wasn't sure if you were a goose or a duck. In the end, I kind of made a lucky guess." She shrugged.

"That's amazing," said Kate. "What did you find in John's sample?"

Dr. Beck looked confused. "John?"

"Yeah, I had two samples done up," said Kate. "One for me, and one for my friend John."

"I must not have found anything," said Dr. Beck, "but let's take a closer look. You sent his in with yours?"

Kate nodded. Dr. Beck clicked through a series of files, finally bringing up John's sample. "Okay, see here?" She pointed to the image of the double helix. "This is your friend's sample. No switch."

"Oh, that's weird," said Kate. "Because he's a werewolf. Or at least, he *was* a werewolf."

Dr. Beck's eyes grew wide. "Are you telling me someone who was a werewolf somehow ceased to be a werewolf?"

"Well, yeah," said Kate. "I mean, it's a long story, but he, like, got shot with a silver bullet and was saved by this potion that had the unfortunate side effect of making him not a werewolf anymore."

Dr. Beck blinked.

"You're going to have to give me the longer version of that."

"Ha, well," said Kate nervously, "we found this old recipe for something called Cure for Werewolf, which we thought would give us a month off of changing. We drank it, and it didn't do anything. Like, nothing. But later on, when John got shot with a silver bullet, his dad took the cure and poured it over the wound. And it was crazy, but it totally saved his life. And now, he's just a regular guy. I mean, he's still a weirdo and everything, but he's not a werewolf anymore."

"This is wild," said Dr. Beck. "I can't imagine how that can be possible. Unless...."

"Unless what?" said Kate.

"Where did you get the recipe?"

"My grandma. It's this super old recipe that's been handed down in her family for, like, ever."

"Would you be able to get me the recipe?"

"Yeah, sure," said Kate. "It's not a big deal to make."

"But it didn't work when you drank it?"

"Nope."

Dr. Beck hopped off her stool and began to pace the floor. "John was shot...so there was trauma?"

"I would say getting shot is pretty traumatic, yeah," said Kate.

"No, I mean, there was a wound? An open wound?"

"Yup," said Kate. "It was awful."

"And the cure was poured directly on the wound?"

Kate nodded.

"Oh my goodness, Kate," said Dr. Beck excitedly, stopping her pacing to look at Kate. "If what you're telling me is true, there's something in the cure that can somehow dissolve the protein switch."

"Then why didn't it work when we drank it?"

"Whatever the active ingredient is must have been destroyed in your stomach by your digestive juices," said Dr. Beck.

"Okay," said Kate.

"But because John's was applied directly to his wound, it was like giving him a needle, directly into his bloodstream. This is incredible! This could change everything."

"What do you mean?"

"It means I can synthesize the Cure for Werewolf. I can make a drug that can be injected into a werewolf that makes them not a werewolf anymore."

Kate thought. "But we kind of already knew how to do that. I mean, this bypasses the whole shot-by-a-silver-bullet phase, but what's the big deal?"

"The big deal is: if we can unlock the mystery of this protein switch, we won't just be able to turn it off. We'll be able to turn it *on*. Kate, we could make someone into a werewolf."

CHAPTER THIRTEEN

JOHN DASHED UP THE STAIRS AT SCHOOL AND down a hallway to his locker. He had only a minute or two to dump his bag and head to his first period class.

He stopped in front of his locker and began to dial in his combination.

"Thirty-two, eighty-five, twenty-nine," came a voice from behind him.

"Quit it," John said, recognizing Jolene's voice right away. He turned the dial twice to the right to reset and begin again. "You're screwing me up."

"What a shame, New Guy," said Jolene, leaning against the locker beside him as he fiddled with the dial. "Nineteen, sixty-seven, two, ninety-one...."

John let go of the lock. "You did it," he said. "I can't remember my combination. Happy now?"

She smiled devilishly. "Ecstatic."

John turned his back on her and walked toward English class.

"Whoa, New Guy," she called, scurrying to catch up. "I didn't realize you were so sensitive."

"And I didn't think you were talking to me anymore, since—"

"Since what, New Guy?"

"Since I discovered your little secret," he said, turning into their classroom as the bell rang. Everyone who wasn't sitting rushed to their seats.

Jolene put her books on her desk and sat down. "I don't have a little secret," she said.

"Right," whispered John as Mr. Scribbage stood up from his desk. "The queen of werewolf haters doesn't keep a shrine to werewolves in her bedroom."

"It's not a shrine," she hissed as the teacher began to talk.

"I know what I saw," John whispered back.

"Settle down, settle down," said Mr. Scribbage as he waited for the class to stop talking. "Okay, this is the day we've been waiting for. Today we start the presentations for your independent study. The first presentation will be by..." He paused as he glanced at a list on his desk. "Jolene and John. Their paper is entitled 'Sparkly Vampires: Not as Horrible as Stupid Werewolves.'" The class snickered. "Sounds enlightening," he said. "John, Jolene, you have the floor."

John put up his hand. "Uh, Mr. Scribbage?" he said. "I've got a little problem."

"And what, pray tell, is that?"

"Well," said John. "I, uh, don't seem to have my presentation with me."

Mr. Scribbage raised his eyebrows. "And where is it?"

"I think it's, uh, in my locker."

"And why is it still in your locker when it is supposed to be here?"

"Well," stammered John. "I guess it's because I, um, couldn't recall my locker combination this morning." He shot a look across the aisle at Jolene, who was smiling sweetly.

The class laughed.

"A presentation locked in a locker," said Mr. Scribbage dryly. "That is unfortunate. Well, then. I'm afraid you'll just have to wing it."

"Wing it?" repeated John.

"Yes, wing it. Is that a problem?"

John looked from his teacher to Jolene, who continued to beam at him. "Uh, no," he said. "Not at all."

John and Jolene stood up and walked to the front of the class. Jolene held a set of cue cards with her presentation notes on them. She looked down, scanned the first few lines, and began to speak.

"Since the first humans gathered around the warmth and protection of a campfire, we have told each other stories," she said. "Stories of people who do odd and even supernatural things. Among the lamest of these stories are those that tell of people who turn into wolves. Werewolves belong to a whiny tradition of—"

John cleared his throat and interrupted. "And yet, our assignment is about vampires, especially the variety who are very, very sparkly. So let's explore some of the ideas of how our attitudes toward these undead creatures have evolved over the years. In this book, the reader must forget the classical understanding of a vampire in order to—"

"*Forget* being the optimal word," injected Jolene, stepping in front of John, "in the same way that my esteemed colleague here has *forgotten* his copy of the presentation in his locker."

The class laughed.

"And so," continued Jolene, "like a defenseless werewolf crying in the night, he must make noise into the still night air, transforming himself into a quivering mass of fur and self-loathing."

"It is, indeed, a remarkable transformation," said John. "Much like the transformation of this presentation about vampires into one about werewolves."

He glared at his partner. What was going on with her? How could a girl with a bedroom shrine to all things werewolf be so weird about werewolves?

Mr. Scribbage cleared his throat. "This presentation has decayed into bickering in record time."

Jolene crossed her arms. "He started it."

"Oh, that's really mature," said John.

"Like howling into the darkness is any more mature."

"Look, I have no idea what kind of—"

The entire class, which until this moment had been mesmerized by what was fast becoming the most interesting presentation it had ever seen, was jolted to attention by a knock at the door. Mr. Scribbage straightened his tie and walked to the door. A pair of police officers was on the other side.

"I'm going to go out on a limb, John," said Mr. Scribbage, turning back to the classroom, "and say these gentlemen are here to see you."

Constable Anderson nodded slightly and beckoned to John with his finger to join them in the hall. John looked from the cops, to Mr. Scribbage, to Jolene—whose smile seemed to indicate she was thoroughly enjoying his torture. He walked to the hallway.

"Look, I realize this may not matter much to you guys," said John, after Mr. Scribbage had shut the door behind them. "But it is extremely hard to make friends at a new school when the cops keep showing up to pull me out of class."

"Gosh," said Dufour in mock surprise, turning to his partner. "That doesn't make sense. Anderson, weren't you under the impression that teens think police officers are cool?"

"That's what I was led to believe," said Anderson. "But John here seems to think hanging out with police officers isn't helping with his popularity. Like, we're *uncool* or something."

"Gotta say, John," said Dufour, crossing his arms. "That stings."

"Okay, okay," said John, leaning against a locker. "Look, I don't know anything more than what I told you last time."

"Oh no?" said Anderson.

"I told you before, I don't know where my dad is."

"Well, that's too bad," said Dufour.

"Too bad, indeed," said Anderson. "Because I know where he is."

John straightened.

"Yeah, me too," said Dufour. "In fact, I saw him about twenty minutes ago. He says hi, by the way."

John blinked. "What are you talking about?"

Dufour grinned. "Hi," he repeated. "You know, like, a friendly greeting?"

"I know what 'hi' means," said John. "Where's my dad?"

Anderson feigned surprise. "Why, jail of course."

CHAPTER FOURTEEN

"BOBBY!" YELLED KATE, MARCHING THROUGH THE house. "Bobby!"

"Where is that kid?" said Lisa, emerging from the kitchen.

"He knows we're leaving this morning," said Kate. "BOBBY!"

Marge walked through the front door. "The van's all packed," she announced. "By the amount of stuff we're bringing, you'd think we were setting up base camp at Everest."

"Grandma, have you seen Bobby?" asked Kate.

Marge scratched her head. "Not for a while," she said. "Can't find him?"

"No, and we've looked everywhere," said Kate.

Kate's grandmother thought for a moment. "Did you check the barn?"

Kate rolled her eyes. "Of course, the barn."

"Gotta get one last session in with his beloved radio, I'd wager," said Marge. "The kid fawns over that old thing like it was his baby. You'd think we hadn't even bought him that small portable one to take on the trip."

"I'll go get him," said Kate. "I'd like to leave today."

Bobby sat with the old headphones clamped to his head, moving the dial slowly up the frequency spectrum. He'd been sitting here for a while, trying to catch the latest broadcast from D-Net. It was supposed to have had a major update on Dirk about ten minutes earlier. But this wouldn't be the first time Shadow, the host of D-Net, missed a broadcast. He was likely in some sort of mortal peril, trying to expose the truth about werewolves and Dirk. He seemed to always be on the run, always on the lookout, always in danger. A little ripple shot up Bobby's spine. It was that exact sort of thing that made listening to D-Net so exciting.

Bobby turned up the gain. Shadow always broadcast at a different frequency, and Bobby didn't want to miss the subtle cues that indicated a broadcast was imminent. He leaned in closer to the machine as he bumped up the gain just a bit more.

"BOBBY, WHAT THE HECK ARE YOU DOING?"

Bobby went cross-eyed as he ripped the headphones from his head. His sister stood beside him, microphone in her hands. She must have snuck up on him.

"Are you trying to kill my ears?"

"Are you trying to make us late for our trip?"

"Oh," said Bobby sheepishly. "Is it time to go?"

"Like five minutes ago," Kate replied.

"Just give me, like, one more minute," said Bobby. He yanked his headphones out of the jack to activate the loudspeaker. "I swear it'll be worth it."

He adjusted the frequency. Squeals and static were suddenly replaced with a woman's voice.

"...*hana, dul, set, net, dausut, ilgup...*" said the voice.

"What's that?" asked Kate. "Some sort of secret code?"

"Nah," said Bobby, adjusting the dial past the voice and into a new set of squeals and static. "It's just some lady counting in Korean."

"Oh yeah," said Kate dryly. "This is really worth my time. Absolutely worth being late for."

"Shhhhh," said Bobby, waving his hand in the air. "D-Net is supposed to have news about Dirk this morning."

Kate scoffed. "Spare me, Bobby. Like I care what a bunch of nerds in their basements think about—"

Kate stopped abruptly as the squealing and static faded away. For a moment, the radio was silent.

"I think this is it!" said Bobby, jumping up and down in his seat.

The speakers began to vibrate with a low-frequency hum. Slowly, the hum moved up the frequency spectrum, becoming so high Bobby had to reach, yet again, to turn down the volume.

When he turned it back up a few seconds later, a robotic voice spoke from the radio.

"That should make sure none of the *freaks* are listening," it said. "You're listening to D-Net. We are your first and last authority on all things werewolf, wereduck, and on the continuing search for the only man brave enough to speak truth to power."

"Whoa," said Kate, dropping into the chair next to her brother.

CHAPTER FIFTEEN

"OKAY, SORRY I'M LATE, EVERYBODY," SAID THE voice. "I want to tell you that I was dodging some government agent or dangling from a helicopter in some sort of narrow brush with death, but the truth is…I cut myself shaving."

Bobby smirked and elbowed Kate in the ribs. "That's Shadow," he said. "He's hilarious."

"Next time, it'll be something way cooler, I promise," said Shadow. "So, I said today we'd have some big news about the one and only Dirk Bragg."

The radio went quiet for a minute.

"Sorry, everyone," said Shadow. "Just tinkering with my encryption. I'm getting some readings that show someone is trying to nail down my broadcast coordinates."

The sound of typing came through the speakers.

"There," said Shadow. "That should do it. Okay, so Dirk. Before I give you the news, I must remind you that many Bothans died to bring us this information."

"That's a *Star Wars* quote," whispered Bobby.

"I know," hissed Kate.

"Just kidding," said Shadow. "But major props go to Symba, Tal-bot, and NinjaGeek29 for their excellent intel. D-Net truly couldn't exist without the hacker chops of the collective. And this was an impressive hack indeed. D-Net can now confirm the NYPD, state police, FBI, and the RCMP have been running a joint investigation on the disappearance of Dirk. We have intercepted encrypted correspondence between all agencies, which put significant resources toward finding Dirk. Like, hundreds of investigators. We've sorted through all the documents and come to two conclusions. Three, actually."

"Bobby, you never told me this was so cool," whispered Kate.

"Shhhhhh!"

"Conclusion number one," said Shadow. "The police don't have a clue. They have no idea what they're doing. Bunch of bumbling bumble-heads, honestly. Conclusion two: any time the police were presented with information that might lead them down a supernatural path—like werewolves—they disregarded it as nonsense. And finally, the most important conclusion: after months of investigating and thousands of man-hours, they're letting the case go cold."

Bobby and Kate gasped.

"Let that sink in for a minute," said Shadow. "The police have decided to stop actively looking for Dirk

Bragg. A guy with a multi-platinum record and two consecutive number-one songs on the music charts. A guy who was dangerously close to bringing the truth about werewolves to the mainstream."

Shadow laughed a bitter, dark laugh.

"Now, the official line is that they are 'investigating some promising leads,' but the reality is: the case is closed. They're going to let this missing person remain missing."

"Good riddance," said Kate.

"Kate!" said Bobby.

"Again," said Shadow, "I want to thank members of the D-Net for this information. Major shouts out to those responsible. If you have details you want to share, and if you know how to get a hold of me, I encourage you to do so. If you don't know how to get a hold of me—" Shadow paused to clear his throat "—tough luck, narc."

"Shadow is so cool," whispered Bobby.

"Members of D-Net, I think we all know what this means," said Shadow. "It's up to us now. We have to find Dirk ourselves. I want no corner of the world left unsearched. Hack into databases. Crack into email servers. If you've looked somewhere and didn't find any useful information, look again. You might have missed something. And even though I know most of you beautiful nerds are locked in basements staring at computer screens, I want you to also use your eyes. Look around. You never know. You just may catch a glimpse of Dirk out there in the wild."

"Please," said Kate, rolling her eyes. "The guy is probably at the bottom of a river."

Bobby shoved her.

"One more thing," said Shadow. "I've had a couple people mention some sort of code word that's popped up a few times in various locations. We can't seem to get a definition for it, as even the FBI seems stumped by what it means exactly. Whatever it is, it is super-secret, and super powerful—powerful enough that it shut down the investigation into Dirk's disappearance. It's called Project Firefly."

"Project Firefly?" repeated Kate.

"So keep your eyes and ears open. Until next time: watch for news of our next broadcast in the usual places. Stay safe, D-Net. Shadow out."

Bobby clicked off the radio.

"Do you really think Dirk's at the bottom of a river?" he asked.

"I dunno," said Kate. "I mean, I don't want that to happen to anybody, but life sure has been a lot easier without Dirt Bag sneaking around."

"I guess," said Bobby, looking thoughtful. "I just hope somebody finds him. I know that guy is a supreme jerk, but everyone in D-Net seems to think he's amazing. And, like, he's the only one who takes stuff like werewolves seriously. No one else seems to want to believe people like us are real."

"Yeah, but he thinks we're real *and* he hates us," Kate reminded him. "There's a difference."

Bobby sighed. "I guess I kind of like the idea of not having to hide all the time."

"Me, too," said Kate. She got up from her chair. "I just seriously doubt Dirt Bag's the guy who's going to make it happen for us. Get your stuff. It's time to go."

CHAPTER SIXTEEN

JOHN JUMPED AT THE HEAVY, METALLIC *CHUNK* AS the door closed behind him.

"Reinforced steel," said Constable Dufour, taking off his mirrored sunglasses. "Wouldn't want anyone having any ideas of escape."

"Right," said John.

He looked around the room. It was long and narrow, with a series of booths along one side. A glass window in each booth looked into a second room, almost identical to this one. "Remind me again why Dad's in this high-security place, when he hasn't been convicted of anything?"

"We got a special court order to keep him here, given his history," said Anderson.

"What history?" said John. "He's never hurt anyone."

"No," said Anderson, "but given the fact he's eluded capture for more than a decade, it wasn't hard to convince the judge he was a flight risk."

John nodded.

A loud *buzzzz* echoed through the room. John saw a set of doors on the other side of the visitation windows open. His dad walked through, escorted by a guard. Marcus's face lit up when he saw his son.

"You've got ten minutes," said Dufour. He picked up a phone receiver hanging on the wall in one of the booths. "You can speak to him through this."

"Thanks," said John, not feeling terribly thankful. He took the receiver.

Marcus slid into the chair opposite John. He picked up his phone.

"Fancy seeing you here," he said.

"Oh, Dad," said John. "What happened?"

Marcus's smile stayed on his face, but John could see him deflate a bit. "I got sloppy is what happened," he said. "You were right. I should have just hit the road and stayed lost."

"Where'd they find you?"

Marcus shrugged. "Does it matter? Not far from your house. I'd been camping in the woods nearby, which was probably another mistake."

"Have they charged you already?"

"Yeah," said Marcus with a chuckle. "The hands of justice move swiftly, I guess. They've had a case ready against me for nearly fourteen years, so putting together kidnapping charges wasn't too difficult."

"What if I told them I didn't mind being kid-napped?" asked John.

"Doesn't matter," said Marcus. "They can just trot out some psychiatrist to say that many victims become naturalized to their situation."

"What about Mum? What if she says she doesn't want to press charges?"

"You're a lot like her, you know," said Marcus. "She, in fact, already did that very thing. They called her right away to let her know I'd been arrested, and she insisted they let me go. But it doesn't work that way."

"What does that mean?"

"It means you've watched too many American crime dramas," said Marcus with a small smile. "Canadian law doesn't require a victim to press charges. All that matters is that a law has been broken."

"But maybe if I testify that—" began John.

"It honestly won't make a difference what you testify," said Marcus, suddenly much more serious. "Whether the court finds me guilty is completely unimportant. Because none of it is going to matter one bit."

"What does that mean?" John said again, fighting back tears.

"It means," said Marcus, "that if I'm still sitting in a jail cell when the moon is full in three weeks' time, no one is going to care about justice." He paused and lowered his voice. "All they're going to care about is that I've suddenly turned into a wolf."

CHAPTER SEVENTEEN

"GRANDMA, KATE'S TOUCHING ME," WHINED Bobby from the back seat of the van.

"I'm literally five feet away from you," said Kate from the front seat. "I'd have to be an acrobat to be able to touch you."

Bobby threw a comic book at his sister. "So?"

"So, I think someone's cranky after seventeen hours in the car," said Kate.

Bobby pulled at his seat belt. He writhed in his seat. "Grandma, I'm so boooored!"

"I feel like dumping you in the middle of the woods to let you walk the rest of the way," said Marge from the driver's seat. "Honestly, we'll be there in a few minutes. Keep your shirt on."

A series of excited quacks erupted from the back of the van.

"Wacka would also like you to keep your shirt on," said Kate.

"I think Wacka might be starting to recognize where we are," said Marge.

"Whoa!" exclaimed Bobby as a rush of feathers whooshed past him.

Wacka flew through the narrow space between the front seats and landed on Kate's lap. She craned her neck to gaze at the blur of trees and rocky terrain out the window. "We're almost there, Wacka!" said Kate. "We're almost home!"

"Wacka," said Wacka.

The little duck was happier than Kate had seen her in months. This trip home, truly, was what she needed—what they all needed. Kate felt a rush of excitement in her stomach at the thought of seeing their old campsite and cabin again.

"Tell me again what Dr. Beck told you," said Marge. "She can make someone *into* a werewolf?"

"Well, not exactly," said Kate. "Not yet anyway. It's kind of complicated, and I'm not sure I entirely get it. But because she now has a chance to get a good look at John's DNA, she thinks she can learn a whole lot more about what makes us different."

"I don't get it," said Marge. "Why is John the key?"

"Because he was a werewolf, but he isn't anymore," said Kate. "So he has all the *stuff* in him to be a were-wolf, but it's been shut off. If she can find the thing that shuts it off, she can, in theory, do all sorts of things."

"Like make new werewolves?" said Marge.

"Maybe," said Kate. "It's all really complicated stuff, even for Dr. Beck. She said it could be a while before she could come up with some way of doing it, but she's just excited to know that it's even possible. What she can do now is figure out what it was that shut off John's werewolf stuff. And maybe even find a way to duplicate it, without the nastiness of being shot with a silver bullet."

"But why do we want that?" said Marge.

Kate shrugged. "Science, Grandma. Haven't you ever wondered about why we're the way we are? There are so many things we don't know. Why are you a werewolf? Why did I become a duck? I'd rather know for sure, rather than just assume it's some sort of magic."

"I just worry," said Marge.

"Why?" said Kate. "None of this is dangerous."

"I don't know," said Marge. "I think it's all dangerous. It's not a bad thing to ask big questions, but if it leads to more people knowing about us, I'm not sure I like where that could lead. Life was awfully quiet when it was just us: our family, alone, in the woods."

"I guess," said Kate. "But wouldn't it be even quieter if you could just take a pill and become a normal person?"

Marge stared at the road. "Is that something you really want?"

Kate looked out her window. "I don't know. Maybe. No. I don't know for sure." She turned to look at her grandmother in the driver's seat. "It's weird, Grandma. I love being a duck. I love being in a family of werewolves. But ever since Dr. Beck said it was possible, I can't stop thinking about it."

Marge reached over to squeeze Kate's knee.

"Well, you're fourteen," said Marge. "Asking questions about who you are is pretty normal." She smiled.

"I'd be a little worried if you thought you had life all figured out by now."

"I have life figured out right now," announced Bobby from the back seat. "I figure, if you haven't got it figured out by ten, there's something wrong with you."

"I stand corrected," said Marge, giving Kate a sly wink.

Wacka interrupted them all with a fresh flurry of quacks.

"You're right, Wacka! This is our road!" said Kate. The tickles in her tummy started again stronger than ever as familiar landmarks whizzed past her window. She never realized how much she missed the backwoods of New Brunswick.

Marge pulled the van into a nondescript driveway bordered by spruce forest. The trees opened on a clearing with a lake on one side and a small cabin on the other.

"Home!" yelled Kate as Wacka squirmed on her lap, eager to fly out the door.

"Wait," said Marge suddenly. "Something's not right."

She put the van in park, cut the ignition, and scanned the campsite. "Someone's been here."

Kate scanned too. The normally neat pile of firewood beside the cabin was depleted to almost nothing. What was left was scattered around the yard. A broken window in the cabin had been patched with an old shopping bag. Empty food cans and wrappers littered the ground.

"We'd better be careful," said Marge. "We've been gone long enough, someone could be squatting here."

Kate gulped. "What should we—"

Kate was interrupted by the slamming of the cabin door. A wild-looking man dashed at the van—his long hair and beard were a tangled mess, and his clothes so dirty it was hard to tell what colour they were.

"TRESSPASSERS!" he shouted. "BE OFF! LEAVE THIS PLACE!"

Kate gasped and locked the doors. Marge restarted the van.

"We're getting out of here," she said. She slid the van into reverse.

"Wait!" said Bobby from the back seat.

The wild man was at the front of the van. He brought down both fists on the hood, making a loud *THUMP*.

"THIS IS PRIVATE PROPERTY, GET OUT! OUT!! OUT!!!" he shouted.

"We ARE getting out!" yelled Marge.

"Grandma, drive!" urged Kate.

"No! Don't!" shouted Bobby. "Don't you see? Look at him!"

Kate looked at the man. He was waving his arms and shouting.

"What else do I need to see?" said Kate. "He's going to kill us!"

"Kate, he won't kill us," said Bobby. "Kate, look! It's Dirk."

CHAPTER EIGHTEEN

JOHN STEPPED OUT THE POLICE STATION'S FRONT doors. The midday sun stung his eyes. He didn't want to go home, but he had no idea where he should go. Usually, when things got tough, John turned to his dad. Only that wasn't an option this time. He could go to Kate, but she was half a country away. He could talk to his mum, but he already felt like he'd done nothing but complicate things for her since he came home.

Three weeks.

It would be three short weeks before everything went to hell for everyone he cared about. Marcus would turn into a werewolf in jail, and the truth about were-wolves (and wereducks) would be out in the open. Who knows what would happen after that?

He wandered around downtown, thinking about everything and nothing. He walked along the waterfront, stopping for a few minutes to watch some ducks dabbling along the muddy shore.

A horrible ball of feelings writhed in his gut. It felt like a physical object. John wished Kate were here. He'd been so lonely since he moved in with his mum. He thought he'd make some new friends at school, but everyone just ignored him because of his constant run-ins with the police. The only person who paid him any attention was Jolene, and, well, he could use a little less of that kind of attention.

He'd been walking around the city for a few hours before he decided to head home. It was still probably a twenty-five-minute walk. His stomach rumbled. He'd been so distracted he forgot he hadn't eaten lunch.

He turned up an unfamiliar side street. He didn't know Moncton very well yet, but he was heading in the right direction. Maybe this street would shave a few minutes from his walk. Maybe, he'd even be in time for—

An old blue cargo van with tinted windows screeched to a halt beside him. The side door slid open with a loud *CHUNK*.

"New Guy," said a voice. "Thank God I found you. Get in."

Jolene beckoned from a bench seat inside the van. A laptop was perched on her knees.

"No thanks," said John. He started walking again.

The van crept forward to keep pace with him.

"Seriously, New Guy," she said. "Get in."

"Jolene, I'm really not in the mood for—"

"Would you just shut up?" interrupted Jolene. "I'm not messing around. You really need to get in the van."

John rolled his eyes. "Look, I don't know what game you're up to today, but—"

"I know about your dad," Jolene blurted out. "And I know what's going to happen in three weeks."

John stopped walking.

"I know everything," said Jolene, looking straight into his eyes. "Everything. Get in. We need to talk."

CHAPTER NINETEEN

"DIRK...BRAGG?" SAID MARGE SLOWLY. HER EYES narrowed as she examined the wild man who was screaming and pounding his fists on the hood of her van.

"Grandma," began Kate. "Grandma, you've got a weird look in your eye. It's freaking me out."

"Well then," said her normally stoic grandmother. She slowly turned to face Kate. "Let's get freaky."

"Grandma!"

Marge opened the door and walked three steps toward Dirk.

"Get your grubby fists off my van," she told him, wagging a finger in his face.

Dirk rounded on her. "Make me, old lady!" he bellowed.

Marge nodded, as if considering his words. Quick as a cat, she swept Dirk's feet from under him with a perfectly timed kick.

"Grandma!" gasped Kate and Bobby in unison as Dirk hit the ground.

"Old lady, am I?" growled Marge through clenched teeth. She pinned him to the ground with a knee on his chest. "You listen to me, Dirk Bragg."

Dirk stammered, but Marge plowed on.

"Oh, yes, I know who you are, you no-good, banana-chomping, tabloid-writing, country-song-twanging *filth*."

"Who," sputtered Dirk, still on his back, "who are you?"

Kate jumped down from the van and strode into Dirk's line of sight. She gave him a little wave.

"Hey."

Dirk's eyes bulged. He looked from Kate to Marge and back again.

"Oh," he said, resigning himself to the situation. "Oh," he repeated, the fight slowly fading from him. "Kate."

He closed his eyes, considering his options. His eyes popped back open. He suddenly looked calm, almost friendly. "Can I offer you some tea or something?"

Kate looked at her grandmother, then back at Dirk. "That would be nice," she said. "Thanks."

CHAPTER TWENTY

JOLENE TYPED AWAY ON HER LAPTOP. SHE HADN'T said a word since John had climbed in the van.

"Thunk, I'm almost ready," she said to her brother, who was in the driver's seat. "Gimme twenty seconds."

Thunk gave her a thumbs-up and punched a few buttons on a custom control panel to the right of the steering wheel.

John looked around. The whole van was decked out with flashing lights, switches, and computer screens. Where the back row of seats would normally be sat a large mass of humming gear. Bundles of wires snaked across the ceiling to control panels and racks of equipment throughout the van. Even the chair-back in front of John was covered with buttons and switches.

"Are you going to tell me what's going on, or—"

"*Shhh*," Jolene said, waving a hand. "I'll explain in a sec." She put on a headset that had been hanging from a clip on the ceiling. She adjusted the microphone to her mouth. "Thunk, I'm good to go. Let's do this." She glanced at John. "Cover your ears for a sec."

Thunk flipped a toggle on the dashboard and gave his sister a nod.

An electronic hum began to vibrate the whole van. It started low and slowly got higher, until it was so high John thought his eardrums would explode.

The humming stopped. Jolene began to speak.

"That should make sure none of the *freaks* are listening," she said into her headset mic. "You're listening to D-Net. We are your first and last authority on all things werewolf, were*duck*, and on the continuing search for the only man brave enough to speak truth to power. A man so dangerous to the status quo, the status quo stole him from us. I'm talking about Dirk Bragg."

"What," whispered John, "is happening?"

CHAPTER TWENTY-ONE

"I, UH, LOVE WHAT YOU'VE DONE WITH THE PLACE," said Kate, looking around the cabin. This little building had been her home for so many years, but now she couldn't believe how small it was. She also couldn't believe how much of a mess Dirk had made of it in less than a year.

Dirk hadn't needed the extra bunks Kate's family had slept in, but neither had he bothered to dispose of them properly. Each bunk had been dragged to a corner of the cabin. A smaller single bed—Bobby's—had been flipped on its side. The normally impeccably swept concrete floor was caked with leaves and dried muddy footprints.

Dirk took the kettle from the stove as it began to whistle. He filled four mugs with hot water.

"Those mugs are clean, are they?" said Marge suspiciously, eyeing the state of the rest of the dirty cabin.

Dirk grabbed one of the mugs. He shut one eye and peered inside.

"Sure," he said.

"Gross," said Bobby, fidgeting on a chair at the table. "I don't want any."

"Give me a little credit," said Dirk. "I may be a slob, but I'm not about to feed you dirty tea."

Bobby crossed his arms. His grandmother shot him a look. "Okay, fine," he conceded. "Thank you."

Dirk placed mugs before each of them. Kate peered in hers and made a face. Bits of twigs and leaves floated on the top.

"Ew," she announced.

"Looks like dirty tea to me, Dirt Bag," said Bobby.

"I knew you were a jerk," said Kate. "But I never knew you were a *gross* jerk."

"Probably trying to poison us," said Bobby.

"Calm down, you two," said Marge, picking up her mug. She gave it a sniff and looked at Dirk. "Birch?" she asked.

Dirk, who until just this moment had looked sheepish, gave a little nod.

"Birch tea can be quite nice, if you know how to make it," she said, blowing on the tea to cool it down. She stirred it a few times and spooned out the leaves, bark, and other floaty bits. She took a sip. "And that's pretty good," she admitted. "I wouldn't have thought to put the bark in, but that's not bad."

"It's supposed to have magnesium and other good stuff in it," said Dirk, sipping from his own mug. "You're a lot nicer when you're not kicking my legs out from under me."

"And you're a lot nicer when you're not trying to put my family on the front cover of your rotten newspaper."

Dirk sighed. "Touché," he said, setting down his mug. "Let's just say my motivations have...shifted...in the last few months."

Kate looked from Dirk to her grandmother to Bobby. "What happened?" she said. "I thought you were a robot programmed to expose werewolves."

"I am," said Dirk. He frowned. "At least I was. But that was before...you know." He took a drink from his mug.

Kate looked awkwardly around the cabin again. "Before what?"

Dirk gave a short, bitter laugh. "Oh, come on," he said. "You know what's happened to me—what I've become."

Kate looked at her brother.

"Awkward," said Bobby.

"What exactly have you become, Dirk?" asked Kate.

"Please!" he shouted, getting up from his chair. "You more than anyone should know! *You* made me like this! You and your disgusting werewolf friends." He nearly spat the last two words. He walked to the window and stared outside. "Though I suppose I deserve it," he added quietly.

"You've got some complicated biz going on in that head, Dirt Bag," said Bobby.

"Dirk, for real," said Kate. "I'm not joking. I'm not being coy. I'm not being *anything.* I have no idea what you're talking about."

Dirk looked back from the window. "You're serious?" he said. "You don't know what happened to me?"

Kate, Bobby, and Marge shook their heads.

"No idea," said Marge.

"On the train," said Dirk. "When you all locked me in the bathroom?"

"Yeah?" said Kate, still not getting it.

"John grabbed me by the ankle to drag me in?" said Dirk.

"Right," said Kate. Her eyes looked blank.

"He bit me," said Dirk.

"Mm-hmm," said Kate, waiting for some sort of revelation.

Dirk sighed in frustration. "Do I need to spell it out? I was *bitten*...by a *werewolf*—"

Bobby gasped.

"—making me—"

"H-holy," stammered Kate.

"—a werewolf, too." finished Dirk. "I am a stinking, dirty, disgusting, no-good werewolf."

The room was a silent as the news sunk in.

"Well, Dirk," said Marge. "I guess I speak for all of us when I say: welcome to the family."

Kate and Bobby roared with laughter.

CHAPTER TWENTY-TWO

"FIRST, AGAIN, I WANT TO THANK THE D-NET community for more of your excellent intelligence. The tips are coming in fast and furious, and honestly, there are too many of you to thank by name. The beautiful nerds who continue to hack their way to the truth know who they are. Thank you, nerds."

John was too stunned to say anything. Had she said Dirk? Bragg? He stared as Jolene plowed on.

"These are dark times, friends," said Jolene into her headset. "As we discussed, law enforcement agencies across North America have given up their search for Dirk Bragg. So we've got that working against us. We're also seeing and hearing more and more references to this so-called Project Firefly, but we're no closer to knowing who or what it is. All we know is Firefly played some role in the next bit of news I'm about to share."

Jolene faced John and looked him in the eye as she spoke.

"Last night, the Royal Canadian Mounted Police in Moncton, New Brunswick, Canada, arrested an important friend of the show. Those of you familiar with the writings of Dirk Bragg will remember the werewolf known as M. Dirk's investigations into M and his son were the closest we've ever come to exposing the truth about werewolves. Well, as I speak, M is sitting in a jail cell, three weeks from the next full moon. I doubt very much I have to remind members of D-Net what will happen to him on the night of the full moon."

John couldn't believe what he was hearing. How was it that Jolene seemed to know so much about him, his father, Dirk, and…everything else?

"Now, you would think I would be delighted by this turn of events," continued Jolene. "Your dedicated host Shadow has been working to expose the truth about werewolves since he could hold a microphone. But, D-Net, forgive me. I believe this news is bad. I believe M has been imprisoned to—"

An alarm buzzed from the control console beside Thunk. He reached over and deftly punched a few buttons as he drove.

"Hold up, D-Net, we've got someone trying to track our signal," said Jolene, cutting her microphone. She was silent for a moment as she typed on her laptop. She clicked and tapped through multiple application windows with dizzying speed.

"What's going on?" asked John.

"Something not good," replied Jolene, not even pausing to look up at him. "Thunk, nothing I'm doing here is working. I keep rotating my encryption, and whoever is tracking us is adjusting just as fast as I am."

Thunk flipped a couple switches on his console and shrugged.

"Okay, you're right," she said. "I'm going to shut it down." Jolene turned her microphone back on. "D-Net, I'm going to have to finish there for the day. Keep your eyes and ears open. Stay safe. Watch for our broadcast in the usual places. Shadow out."

She switched off her microphone and ripped off the headset. "Dammit, Thunk," she said. "I thought we had worked on the rotating encryption generator, but whoever was tracking us was adjusting so fast. It's almost as if they were—"

But Thunk was looking in the rear-view mirror. His eyes were huge.

"What is it, dude?" she asked. "What's up?"

Thunk pointed with his thumb out the back window. Jolene and John swivelled to look.

A grey sedan was driving about two car lengths behind the van.

"Holy crud," said Jolene.

"What's the big deal?" said John. "It's just a car."

"It's not just a car," said Jolene. "Look at the hardware on top of that thing."

John looked again. On the roof of the car were three long antennas and a series of shorter ones.

"So what, they've got a killer CB radio," said John. "What is happening?"

"Turn everything off," said Jolene, flipping every switch she could reach. She powered off her computer. "Thunk, shut it all down."

Thunk flipped a series of switches along his console.

"New Guy, turn off that switch there," said Jolene. "The one with the green light."

"I still don't get—"

"Just do it! Thunk, can you lose these guys?"

He nodded.

"Good," she said, taking a quick look behind them. "Let's do it sooner rather than later."

"Can I interrupt?" said John. "What the *heck* is going on here?"

"Oh, New Guy," said Jolene. "Of course. This is probably all super weird to you. There's so much to tell you."

"Yeah," said John incredulously. "First off, you want to let me know how it is my werewolf-hating friend is suddenly hosting some sort of secret—"

Jolene put up a hand. "I'll tell you everything, I promise. It's just...." She reached forward to tap her brother on the shoulder. "Thunk, that roundabout is coming up—the weird one with the bridge and underpass. You thinking what I'm thinking?"

He flashed her a thumbs up.

"Right on, dude," she said. "We got this. Keep it calm and cool until then. Don't let on that anything's up."

Thunk signalled to enter the right lane, indicating he'd be taking the first exit off the roundabout. The grey car behind them did the same.

"Awesome," said Jolene. "Now time this carefully."

Thunk's eyes narrowed as he tightened his grip on the steering wheel. He drove into the exit lane. The sedan followed.

"Okay, now!" shouted Jolene.

At the last second, Thunk hauled the wheel hard to the left, narrowly missing the concrete support beam holding up the overpass above them. The driver of the sedan didn't have time to react and kept straight through the exit.

"Okay, go, go, go, go, go!" shouted Jolene. "Quick, before he can come back around!"

Traffic going under the overpass ground to a halt. John could no longer see the grey car, but it had clearly stopped midway through the exit and was blocked from turning around by the line of cars behind it.

Thunk re-entered the roundabout and took the second exit. He sped off and cut immediately into a residential area.

"There!" said Jolene, pointing to a house on the left. "That driveway wraps around the house. We can hide behind."

Thunk drove in behind the house. He shut off the engine. All was quiet.

"I don't think they saw which exit we took," whispered Jolene. "We could have gone in one of five directions. If we lie low here for a few minutes, I think we'll be good. All the gear is shut down, so we shouldn't be giving off any residual signal for them to trace."

"Can you tell me what is going on now?" demanded John. "What are we doing? Who was following us? What—" he gestured at all the electronic gear around him "—*is* all this?"

"Absolutely, New Guy," said Jolene. "You deserve answers. But first, we need to get out of here."

"Nope, I need answers," said John firmly. "Like, now. I thought you were a werewolf hater!"

Jolene sighed. She shook her head.

"I knew it," said John. "It's an act."

"I've been obsessed with them since I was a little kid," admitted Jolene. "And, like, with all this—" she gestured at the broadcast equipment "—I can't exactly walk around with *I LOVE WEREWOLVES* on my T-shirt. Gotta keep a low profile. D-Net—sorry, the online group of fans of my show—has been really important. We've discovered some crazy things. Including that your dad is in jail. Which sucks." She gulped. "Big time."

Jolene was looking straight into John's eyes. He was shocked to note there wasn't a trace of sarcasm there.

"Big time," repeated John.

"Which is why we need to leave," she said. "Like, get out of town. There's no way we can make a plan to break your dad out of prison with the cops knocking on your door every few days."

"We're going to...*what*?"

"You heard me. Unless you want the whole world to know he's a werewolf. Look, New Guy. We can do this. It's going to be insanely hard, but I know we can do it." She tapped her laptop. "And we're not alone. We have friends who can help. We just need a spot to lie low and plan this out."

John's head spun. There was too much happening too fast. But Jolene was right. About all of it. He took a deep breath.

"I think I know a place," he said.

CHAPTER TWENTY-THREE

KATE LEANED BACK AND FELT THE SUN DRENCH her face. It had been so long since she had done this—sit on a rock beside her favourite lake and just…be.

She opened her eyes and scanned the sky. At the edge of her vision, over the tops of the spruce forest, a fluttering speck was coming closer. She heard the speck give a faint quack. Kate smiled. Wacka was enjoying being home just as much as Kate was.

A few hundred feet out, Wacka stopped flapping to glide the rest of the way in. Her feet touched the water and skied on the surface for just a moment before vanishing beneath her in the lake. The little duck bobbed happily on the water, her wings folded neatly on her back.

"We're hoooome!" shouted Kate.

"Wacka," quacked Wacka, splashing happily.

Kate smiled.

"I still can't believe you *talk* to a *duck*," said a voice behind her.

Kate's smile melted as Dirk appeared on the rock beside her.

"And I still can't believe you think Big Foot is real and aliens want to suck our brains," she said flatly.

Dirk rolled his eyes. "Aliens don't want to suck our brains," he said quietly. "They want to suck our bank accounts."

"Whatever," muttered Kate.

Dirk and Kate sat in silence as Wacka paddled across the lake toward them. She waddled out of the water and made for their spot on the rock.

"Nice ducky," said Dirk awkwardly, reaching out a hand to pet her.

Wacka hissed.

Dirk's hand shot back. "Whoa!" he said. "I thought you said this duck was friendly."

"No," said Kate, as Wacka climbed on her lap and snuggled in. "I said this duck was smart."

Wacka kept a suspicious eye on Dirk as Kate gently stroked her back.

"This whole thing is blowing my mind," said Dirk.

Kate looked at him. "That's…surprising, actually."

"What do you mean?"

"Well, I mean, you're Dirk Bragg." Kate shrugged. "You're, like, the guy who believes in everything. Conspiracies. Ghosts. Vampires. Martian circus performers—"

"Those guys are the *worst*."

"But also werewolves," continued Kate. "If you believe in all that stuff, how could this," she motioned around her, "blow your mind?"

"I guess it's a different thing to believe in something than to actually *be* it," he said.

Kate nudged Wacka off her lap and stood up. "Careful, Dirt Bag," she said, dusting off her jeans with her hands. "That almost sounds like personal growth."

"Well, don't expect me to howl 'Kumbaya' at the next full moon," muttered Dirk.

Kate smirked. "That's too bad," she said. "Because I have it on pretty good authority you're an okay singer."

Dirk sat up straight. "I mean," he said slyly, "I'm okay. I mean, I've had a few hits."

Kate rolled her eyes and stood up. "Come on, Dirk," she said. She held out her hand to help him up. "You can give me a hand stacking firewood for Grandma."

CHAPTER TWENTY-FOUR

"UH, WE'RE IN THE MIDDLE OF NOWHERE, NEW Guy," said Jolene. "When I said we needed to lie low, I didn't mean fall off the edge of the planet."

Since John directed them off the highway ten minutes ago, the roads had gotten smaller and smaller, until they turned onto what seemed more like a mud track running through the New Brunswick wilderness than an actual road.

"We're going in the right direction," said John, eying the path ahead. "Turn right here."

Thunk wrenched the wheel to the right. Branches scraped the side of the van.

"And this place we're going," said Jolene. "It's safe? We can trust these people?"

John smiled. "A hundred percent. These people are the best."

"And they're going to be cool with us just dropping in unannounced?"

"They'll be fine," said John. "They just got here two days ago. Kate texted when they arrived. They'll probably be glad for some help cleaning up the campsite."

"Oh great," said Jolene. "Manual labour."

Thunk grunted from the front seat.

"Exactly," replied Jolene.

They all stared out the window silence for a few minutes as the van bumped along.

"Okay, this is it," he said, leaning forward. "Turn here."

Thunk turned into a driveway. The lane opened up into a clearing with a cozy cabin on one side and a small lake on the other. A teenaged girl looked up from her work at the woodpile when the van drove in.

"There she is!" said John. "That's Kate!"

John jumped out. "Don't worry!" he yelled. "It's just me. I brought friends."

Kate dropped a split piece of wood onto the pile. "John!" She ran at him at full speed and nearly toppled him over with a giant hug.

"Oof!" said John. "I missed you, too!"

"What're you doing here, you stupid oaf?" laughed Kate. "This is so great! I didn't think we'd see you for weeks!"

"Ha, funny thing, that," said John. "I'll tell you all about it, but first, let me introduce—"

"Hey," said Jolene, standing right beside them.

"Oh," said Kate, startled. "Hi." She blinked and stared at Jolene. She finally stuck out a hand to shake. "I'm Kate."

"Yeah, I know," said Jolene, ignoring the hand.

Kate stood with her hand out for another second before awkwardly retracting it. "And you are?"

"Jolene," blurted Jolene.

Kate looked blank.

Jolene looked at John. "You didn't mention me?"

"W-well," stammered John. "No. But in my defense, until a few hours ago, you were just the weird girl who screwed up my English presentation."

"Fair enough," said Jolene with a nod. She looked around. "Nice place."

Kate couldn't tell if Jolene was being sarcastic. "Thanks."

"So, do you guys, like, have Wi-Fi here or—"

Jolene was interrupted by a deep cough. She turned and found her brother standing beside her. She cocked her head to one side. Thunk was doing something she'd not seen him do since they were little kids.

He was smiling. Beaming, even. At Kate. He cleared his throat.

"Oh," said Jolene. "This is my brother, I guess. Thunk."

"Thunk?" repeated Kate, reaching out a hand to shake his. "Is that your name?"

Thunk furrowed his brow for a moment and nudged his sister with his elbow. She looked at him.

"What?" Jolene said. "What is up with you?"

Thunk coughed and motioned to Kate with his eyes.

"Oh jeesh," she said, finally understanding. "His real name is Alex."

"Alex?" repeated Kate.

Thunk's grin stretched from ear to ear.

"Yeah, but we haven't called him that since he was eight years old," said Jolene, staring hard at her brother.

"Can he…talk?" asked Kate. Her eyes darted between Thunk and Jolene.

"Oh, he can talk," said Jolene. "He just…doesn't."

"Okay," said Kate. "Well, nice to meet you, Thunk."

He frowned.

"Alex," Kate corrected. "Nice to meet you, *Alex*."

Thunk blushed. Kate blushed right back.

"You're weirding me out, Thunk," said Jolene. "I've never seen you go gaga over—"

"Kate!" called a man's voice from behind the cabin. "I found a nice dry log we could split for firewood. If you could help me drag it up here…." Dirk walked around the corner of the cabin. "Oh," he said, startled by the crowd. "I didn't know we were expecting visitors."

Jolene spun around. The man was dirty and dishevelled, but she would recognize that face anywhere. She'd been a fan since she was ten years old. When all her friends had posters of the latest singing sensation, she had cut out his photo from pages of *Really Real News*.

"Dirk…Bragg?" she managed.

"That's me," said Dirk with a smile.

Jolene fainted.

CHAPTER TWENTY-FIVE

WHEN JOLENE CAME TO, JOHN'S JACKET WAS balled up under her head as a pillow. Someone had moved her to the shade of a tree near the cabin.

"There you are," said Marge, who had taken charge the moment she came across the scene. "Welcome back. Can you sit up to drink? I've got some water for you."

Jolene nodded weakly. The older women handed her a tin cup of water. Jolene took a sip.

"How's that?" said Marge, smiling at her. "Better?"

"Yes. Thank you," said Jolene, propping herself up to a sitting position. "Sorry about that."

"Oh, don't apologize," said Marge. "It happens to the best of us. It's Jolene, is it? John introduced us a moment ago, but you didn't seem to be conscious at the time. I'm Marge. Kate's grandma."

Jolene blushed. "Yeah," she said. "Nice to meet you. It was just, for a second, I thought I saw...someone.

Gave me a little shock." She shook her head. "But it couldn't have been."

"Couldn't have been who?" said Dirk, stepping out from behind Marge.

Jolene's eyes grew huge. Her breathing became heavy.

"D-D-D...," stammered Jolene. "Dirk...Bragg?"

"The one and only," said Dirk with a grin. "At least, I used to be. Sorry, do we know each other?"

"D-D-D-D..."

Dirk tilted his head to one side. "Is she all right?"

"She's..." began John. "I don't know how to say this, Dirk. She's a big fan of your writing."

"Oh," said Dirk brightly. "Well!"

John looked back to Jolene, whose eyes seemed to have grown three times their regular size at the sight of her hero. "A *really* big fan."

"Always nice to make the acquaintance of a lover of good journalism," said Dirk, puffing up. "Nice to meet you, Jolene." He extended a hand.

"D-D-D..." was all she could manage.

"Gosh, I hope that gets better," Dirk said with concern. He turned to John. "Oh!" he gasped, realizing for the first time who he was speaking to. His face darkened. "Oh," he repeated. "You."

John stepped closer to Dirk. "Yup," he said, his eyes level with Dirk's. "Me."

"Don't you have a fire hydrant to sniff or something?" said Dirk.

"Don't you have some lives to ruin or something?" said John.

"Ruined lives!" repeated Dirk. "Let's talk about ruined lives, shall we? Let's talk about mangy were-wolves who spread their filthy disease to poor, unsuspecting victims with a bite to the ankle that nearly—"

"Or how about we talk about constantly living on the run, never being able to call one place home for longer than two weeks?" growled John. "My dad's in jail because of you. You're the one who—"

"Hold on, hold on," said Kate, pushing between them. She turned to John. "Your dad's in jail?"

"Yup!" John said, staring at Dirk. "And guess whose stories led the police right to him? He's going to turn into a wolf in the middle of a jail cell, and we'll all be screwed."

"Oh, so it's *my* fault for reporting the truth," said Dirk. "That's pretty rich."

"Stop it!" said Kate, holding them apart with a hand on each of their chests. "We all need to be friends here. Look, there's a lot of stuff that's happened, but we can either dwell on it and hate each others' guts, or we can get over ourselves and be civilized people."

"Like I'm going to be civil to that mangy mutt," spat Dirk.

"Well, what a shame, because I probably couldn't be civil to a sleazebag like you."

"Okay, okay," said Kate. "I see we've got a bit of catching up to do. Both of you are a bit behind the times anyway. And, much as I hate to admit it, having spent time with both of you, I can say you are both—" she cast an apprehensive eye at Dirk "—perfectly nice."

Dirk and John stopped pushing toward each other.

"Kate, what?" said John.

Kate rolled her eyes. "Dirk can be, at times," she looked back and forth between them, "fairly tolerable."

Dirk smiled at her. "You mean it?"

"When you're not trying to put my family in your dumb paper," Kate said, driving an accusing finger into his chest. "Yes."

"Whoa," said John and Dirk together.

"And John, you should probably know," said Kate, thrusting her hands in her jeans pockets, "Dirk is a werewolf now."

John took a step back. "He's a what?"

"A *werewolf*," repeated Dirk.

"And John," said Kate, looking away. "You might've, maybe, made him that way."

"I *what*?" said John.

Dirk nodded.

"I don't understand," said John.

"You honestly don't remember?" asked Dirk.

"Remember what?" John shot back.

"You bit him," said Kate. "On the train. Remember?"

John's eyes went wide. "Oh, my God."

"Yeah," she said.

"Oh, my God," repeated John. "I can't...believe...." He threw back his head and laughed.

"Oh, perfect," said Dirk bitterly as John's guffaws rang through the clearing. "Yeah, laugh it up, wolfy boy."

John's cheeks hurt from laughing so hard. He bent over, trying to calm himself. "But that's the thing!" he gasped, leaning against a tree for support. "You're a wolf. And I'm...I'm...."

His laughter started all over again.

"What is this dude's deal?" said Dirk.

"What he's trying to tell you," said Kate, "is he's *not* a werewolf. Not anymore."

"Oh!" said Dirk in surprise. "Oh," he repeated more seriously. "But how?"

"It's kind of a long story," said John, laughing.

"Try me," said Dirk. "Let's say I have a special interest in any story which ends with someone being cured of this—" he motioned at himself "—affliction."

"Hold up," said Jolene, struggling to her feet. "You're telling me Dirk Bragg—the world's foremost authority on werewolves and werewolf conspiracy—is now a werewolf?"

Dirk sighed. "Pretty much."

"And you don't *want* to be a werewolf?"

"'Fraid not."

"But why not?"

Dirk rolled his eyes. "Because I'm not a freak."

Marge stepped forward. "Okay," she said. "That's enough. Kate's right." She peered around the group. "You are all perfectly nice people, who for some reason can't stop calling each other names."

"He started it," muttered Dirk.

"I did not, you dirty—" spat John.

"*Enough*," repeated Marge. "We have one fairly pressing issue to deal with. If John's dad is indeed in jail, and he's going to turn into a wolf at the full moon, it will expose us all."

"The whole world will know there are werewolves," said John. "None of you will ever be safe."

"Exactly," said Marge. "So I would think it would be in all of our best interests to find a way to get him out of there. Dirk, I'm sorry you're a werewolf, but you have to deal with it. It's not something we can fix."

Dirk crossed his arms.

Kate thought for a moment. "Or maybe it is," she said quietly.

Everyone turned to look at her.

"Maybe we can save John's dad and cure Dirk at the same time," said Kate. She looked at each of them. "But we'd have to work together. All of us."

"I'm not risking jail for the sake of Marcus," said Dirk, shaking his head. "Count me out."

"Oh, I have a better plan for you," said Kate with a smirk. "I think you're going to like it."

CHAPTER TWENTY-SIX

COUNTRY SINGER EMERGES FROM SELF-IMPOSED EXILE, ANNOUNCES MEGA-CONCERT

*Country singer/tabloid journalist Dirk Bragg
to perform at giant venue in Canada*

MONCTON, NEW BRUNSWICK, CANADA—IN A MOVE
that is making waves in the normally disparate worlds
of popular country music and tabloid journalism, Dirk
Bragg, a man missing for nearly a year and thought by
many to be dead, has emerged from hiding to announce
a giant concert in Moncton, New Brunswick, Canada.

Bragg, a longtime journalist for the tabloid newspaper *Really Real News,* made an unexpected career
shift last year when he released a solo country album.

Tabloid Blues is an eclectic mix of banjo-infused country songs about life reporting on aliens and werewolves, the joys of eating a perfectly ripe banana, and Bragg's peculiar brand of ennui. The album left critics scratching their heads, but made fans scream for more. It went quintuple platinum within two months of its release and spawned a half-dozen chart-toppers, including "A Bunch of Bananas (and This Lonely Heart)"; "Dig this Scoop"; "I'm not an Alien (to this Feeling of Desolation)"; "Conspiracy Theory"; "Put the Gun Down, Monkey"; and his signature hit, "My Wheels Belong to the Road (But my Heart Belongs to You)."

Almost as baffling as Bragg's meteoric rise to fame was the parallel mystery of his sudden disappearance. Bragg went missing shortly after the album's release, which spawned numerous conspiracy theories about where he had gone and whether he had gone willingly.

In a statement released yesterday, Bragg claims to have taken a break from the public eye because the express rocket to fame was "too much, too soon for a humble journalist who just wanted to sing a few songs." Bragg says it has now become clear, however, that "fame is something I'm going to have to live with. My fans have been patient and loyal and deserve the best I can give them. This is why I'm going to give the biggest concert ever in two weeks' time at Magnetic Hill. It will be a night to remember, I promise."

Magnetic Hill is a tourist attraction just outside of Moncton, New Brunswick, named after a stretch of rural road, featuring an optical illusion that causes vehicles to appear to roll uphill. The site is also renowned venue for giant concerts, hosting appearances over the years by bands such as U2 and the Rolling Stones, and even an open-air mass presided over by Pope John Paul II. Bragg's appearance is expected to push the concert site's capacity of 100,000 people to its limit.

Bragg appears to be tipping his cap to some conspiracy theorists who believe the government is attempting to silence his reporting on the existence of werewolves. The comeback concert will be July 9—the night of the full moon.

CHAPTER TWENTY-SEVEN

"YOU PROMISED HIM *WHAT*?" SAID THE VOICE ON the phone.

"Um, well, it's kind of complicated," said Kate.

"Complicated?" said Dr. Beck from her office. "I'm a PhD, Kate. Try me."

"I maybe told Dirk you could make him, like, a cure," said Kate.

Dr. Beck said nothing for a long time.

"But only because, Dr. Beck, you're such a *brilliant* scientist. And I know you said it was technically possible, even though you said it would take a lot of time to come up with a specific formula to make it happen—"

"Kate."

"—and I know *technically* I promised him something pretty crazy and maybe even impossible—"

"*Kate.*"

"—but I guess I didn't know what else to do because John's dad is like, in jail, and that's extra awful because if he's still there on the full moon—"

"Kate!"

Kate winced. "Sorry."

"Kate," repeated Dr. Beck. "I think I can help you."

Kate gasped.

"*Maybe*," cautioned Dr. Beck. "I'm giving you a strong maybe here."

"You have a cure ready?"

"Not exactly," said Dr. Beck. Kate could hear her adjust the phone on her ear and tap away at a keyboard. "I've been fiddling around with some of the sequences I found in your friend's DNA. Remember that switch I was telling you about?"

"Yes!"

Kate was over the moon that her gamble just might pay off. In order to break Marcus out of jail, they'd need a distraction—something huge. An idea had popped into Kate's head that even she had to admit was perfect: Dirk could give a giant concert. Fans would flock from the four corners of the earth to see him perform.

Convincing Dirk to do this had been the tricky part, which was where Kate might've overplayed her hand. She had promised him a cure—a potion that would make him fully human again. Even though it was something she didn't *technically* have.

"Kate, are you listening?" said Dr. Beck.

"Sorry, Dr. Beck, I just got a bit excited. What were you saying?"

"It turns out there really was something to that old cure of your grandma's. I prepared the recipe and examined the compounds. There's a lot going on there, chemically speaking. A lot of interactions I wouldn't have imagined. But the real magic happens when you add silver."

Kate gasped. "The silver bullet!"

"Exactly. But it turns out you don't actually need to get shot for it to be effective. If the numbers I'm looking at are correct, I think I could synthesize a cure."

"When?" blurted Kate.

"A month?" guessed Dr. Beck. "Maybe two?"

Kate's stomach dropped. "A *month*?"

"At the earliest."

"So when you say 'a month,'" said Kate, "do you mean, like—"

"A month," said Dr. Beck firmly.

"Is this like on *Star Trek*, when the captain is like, 'yo, Engineering. I need that warp engine back online.' And Engineering is like, 'it's going to take ten minutes.' But the captain says, 'make it two minutes,' and they do it in two?"

A long silence came back down the phone line.

"Maybe you don't like *Star Trek*?" squeaked Kate.

"Of course I like *Star Trek*!" said Dr. Beck. "I just need you to know, this type of genetic work isn't quick or easy. To rush a cure could be very dangerous. Even deadly."

"Deadly?"

"This stuff isn't a game, Kate," said Dr. Beck. "This is fundamentally altering the DNA of a human being. I'm hesitant to even say I can do it, because ethically—"

"But, like, what about the ethics of exposing the truth about werewolves to the whole world?" said Kate. "If Marcus is still in jail when the full moon comes out, that's it. It's over. For all of us. Who knows what the police, the government, or anyone might do if they find out werewolves are real?"

Dr. Beck sighed. "I know. Okay. I'll try to get it to you before the concert."

Kate yelped. "Really?"

"But I make no promises," said Dr. Beck quickly. "So you better have a plan B to make this whole thing work without a cure, okay?"

"Okay, Dr. Beck," said Kate. "You're the best! Thank you so much."

"It's all right," said Dr. Beck. She looked around her lab. She had a huge job ahead of her. "Just, one more thing."

"What is it?"

"I know this is controversial, but no matter what anyone says, *Voyager* was the best *Star Trek*."

"Oh, my gosh, *yes*," said Kate.

"I mean, people talk a lot about the depth of *Deep Space Nine*, but there is just something spectacular about that scrappy little ship trapped on the other side of the universe."

"And Captain Janeway was—"

"—the best captain," finished Dr. Beck. "Hands down."

"Yes, Dr. Beck," said Kate. She closed her eyes and nodded. "Yes."

CHAPTER TWENTY-EIGHT

"I STILL DON'T KNOW HOW YOU EXPECT TO BE ABLE to do all of this, Jolene," said John. He poked at the campfire with a stick. "So much of this plan depends on...whatever it is you do."

Jolene didn't look up from her laptop. The screen gave her face a cold, blue glow. "Don't worry about it," she said. "It'll work fine."

Kate looked around the fire. The whole group was assembled—John, Jolene, Thunk, Bobby, Dirk, and Marge—to go over the plans for the night of Dirk's concert.

"Can you just give me a bit of detail?" said John. "I mean it's not that I don't trust you. It's just—this is my dad we're talking about. I don't want to leave any of this stuff to chance."

Jolene sighed and looked up from her screen. "Okay, New Guy, look," she said. "Everyone has a job to do here, and everyone uses the tools they have to accomplish them. We need a giant diversion, so Dirk is going to give us the biggest diversion ever."

Dirk was scratching in a notebook with a stubby pencil. He looked up at the mention of his name. "Do you think I should start with 'Newsroom Blues' and then go straight into 'My Wheels Belong to the Road,' or should I save that for the encore?"

"Definitely encore," said Jolene, offhandedly. She turned back to John. "We need a dose of Cure for Werewolf to make sure Dirk doesn't transform in front of a crowd of a hundred thousand people, so Ducky's pulling some strings with the science community to make it happen."

"Hey!" said Kate.

Jolene ignored her. "And you need *me* to distract the Project Firefly weirdos and disable the security systems at the prison so Marcus can escape." She shrugged. "No problem. I got this."

She looked back to her laptop and started typing.

"Yeah, okay, but, I guess what I'm wondering is… *how* do you 'got' this?" said John.

Jolene looked up. "With the tools I have at hand," she said, as if it were the most obvious thing in the world. "D-Net. I have access to hundreds of nerds all over the world. They could hack their way in and out of that prison no problem. Marcus will have a red carpet from his cell door to the outside world."

John looked skeptical.

"Trust me!" she insisted. "Okay, look." She turned back to her laptop and started typing. "Okay, I'm chatting with someone named Tal-Bot. She's a longtime D-Net fan."

"Where is she?" asked John.

"I dunno," said Jolene. "Who cares? The internet. Anyway, check this out."

The chat window was replaced by an intricate spreadsheet. Names, numbers, and times were sprinkled throughout.

"This is the duty roster for the jail your dad is in," she said. "Tal-Bot hacked into their HR intranet site, so we can see when the shifts start, when they end, and all sorts of useful stuff so we can time his breakout down to the second."

"Cool," said John.

"And the Firefly weirdos?" said Kate. "I mean, we don't even know who they are, let alone what they want. How are we going to take care of them?"

Jolene continued typing.

"And how do you have Wi-Fi in the middle of the forest?" said Kate.

Jolene sighed and closed the laptop. "There's internet everywhere, if you know where to look for it," she said. "As for Firefly, what do we know about them? They're interested in werewolves. They seem especially interested in the activities of Dirk." She looked at Dirk.

"Banjo," muttered Dirk as he scribbled in his notepad. "I'll have to make sure the band has a banjo player."

"And they've gotten real close to tracking my D-Net broadcasts."

"Which makes them extra dangerous," said Marge. "They could spoil this whole rescue."

"We'll just give them something more alluring to spoil," said Jolene with a grin. "Thunk and I are going to broadcast from the concert. They'll be so distracted by me yammering on about Dirk conspiracy theories, they won't even notice what's happening in the background. And I've worked out a code with some of my best hackers. Some of the lines I say will be triggers for them to disable different parts of the security system at the prison. It's easy-peasy."

"Okay," said John. "I don't fully get it, but I'm going to trust it."

"Good boy," said Jolene.

"Kate," said John. "You and I will be camped out by the jail to help Dad when he gets out."

"What about me?" asked Bobby.

"You're going to be at the concert," said Marge. "With Dirk on stage, Jolene in the crowd, and Thunk manning the broadcast in the van, we'll need someone quick and nimble who can move about freely."

"Got it," said Bobby. "What about you, Grandma? What are you going to be doing?"

Marge looked at Dirk. He was massaging his neck just below his jaw and doing vocal warm-up exercises. He kept saying "wuuaaaah, wuaaaah."

Dirk looked up. Everyone was looking at him.

"What?" he said. "Gotta keep my vocal chords limber."

"I'll have the hardest job of all," said Marge. "Managing the celebrity."

CHAPTER TWENTY-NINE

JOLENE AND JOHN SAT IN PLASTIC CHAIRS IN THE visiting room at the jail. The fluorescent lights hummed.

"Do you think the cops will listen to our conversation?" said John.

"I figure they've got an ear on that," said Jolene, pointing to the phone through which visitors could speak with prisoners on the other side of the glass.

"Then how do we let him know—"

"Just leave it to me."

An electronic *buzzz* let them know the door was being unlocked on the other side of the glass. Marcus emerged and walked toward the chair opposite them. John thought he looked tired. He picked up the phone.

"Hiya, Dad," he said. "You look good."

"Don't lie," said Marcus with a bit of his old twinkle in his eye. "I haven't been sleeping much."

"Pretty rough in there?"

Marcus shrugged. "It's not exactly the place I want to be right now." Marcus nodded at Jolene. "Who's this? Your girlfriend?"

"Oh, God no," said John, thankful Jolene didn't have an ear on the conversation. "She's my friend Jolene. I wanted her to talk to you about something."

Marcus raised his eyebrows. "Okay," he said. "Listen, not that it matters much, but the lawyer they assigned me has actually done some pretty fantastic work. He's struck a deal with the Crown, if you and your mum agree to testify on my behalf."

"Whoa," said John. "So what does that mean?"

"It means, in a normal world, after we have a chance to sit in front of a judge to put a stamp on the deal, I get out of here with just a year of probation." Marcus gave a slow blink. "Too bad it isn't a normal world."

"How long before you can see a judge?"

"A month."

"So that's useless."

"Yup," said Marcus. "*Whoooooooooo!*" he howled softly. "A little too late for my hairy problem next week."

"Right," said John. "Well, about that."

John stared into his dad's eyes. He knew he couldn't say what he wanted. He wanted to say they had a plan to get him out. He wanted to tell him not to worry. He wanted his dad to know he would always be there for him.

He tried to say all of this with a look.

John blinked. "Here's Jolene," he said.

Jolene grabbed the phone from John.

"Hey," she said.

"Hello," said Marcus.

"How are you? I mean, it sucks, right? Jail."

Marcus smirked. "Yeah, I guess you could say that," he said. "Sucks."

"Bummer. Listen, I just want you to know, the weather forecast for the full moon looks really good."

He looked at her.

"Yeah," she said. "My brother is, like, an astrologer? Anyway. He's really into that kind of stuff. I'm just saying: it's going to be a great night for paying close attention to the moon."

"Okay," said Marcus, trying to understand.

"And, like, I'm not into this weird new-agey stuff or anything, but they say weird stuff happens on a full moon. It's just a great idea to pay attention to everything."

"Right," said Marcus, sitting suddenly very straight.

"I just find there's a really cool energy on full moon nights," said Jolene. "Just, like, really free, you know?"

"I think I do."

"Yeah, cool, okay," said Jolene. "Anyway. Prison. Yuck." She blew a raspberry and gave him a thumbs-down.

"Big time," agreed Marcus. "Listen, Jolene, it was nice to meet you."

"Cool. Here's John."

She thrust the phone back at John. He pulled the receiver to his ear.

"So," said Marcus. "That was...interesting."

"I hope you got something out of it," said John.

Marcus nodded. "Oh, yes."

"Good. We're going to be super busy for the next little bit," said John. "So I probably won't be able to visit again soon. But I assume I'll see you next week. Shortly after the full moon."

"Count on it," said Marcus.

CHAPTER THIRTY

"I DON'T KNOW WHY WE NEED TO EVEN HAVE A press conference," said Dirk. "The concert is already sold out. More than a hundred thousand tickets sold! We don't need any more publicity. This thing is a hit before it even starts."

He stood in a back hallway of a convention centre, talking to Marge. She had traded her usual khaki shorts and plaid shirt for a smart-looking dark suit and a pair of wire-rimmed glasses. Her normally frizzy, flyaway hair was tied back in a smart bun.

"Well, first of all," said Marge, "the record label wants you to do this. You've got a lot bigger audience out there than just these hundred thousand fans. And there's an entire music industry that wants answers to where you've been and what you've been up to."

"Okay, granted, but—"

"Second," interrupted Marge, "we need this show to be bigger than big. We need all eyes on you. If our plan to free Marcus is going to work, we need every person on the planet to be paying attention to you. Think you can handle that?"

Dirk shivered. "Oh, my," he said. "I think so."

"Right now, you're the biggest thing going," said Marge. "Even people who hate country music are intrigued by...whatever it is you do. Suddenly popping up after completely vanishing for most of a year seems to have skyrocketed you to mega-stardom."

"Goodness," said Dirk. "Would you say I'm bigger than Beyoncé?"

"Let's not go crazy."

A short man in a grey suit burst through a doorway. Marge recognized him as the manager of the conference centre.

"They're chomping at the bit!" he said excitedly. "I've never seen anything like it. There's all the usual local media, but CNN is here! Even *The New York Times* sent someone!"

"Really?" said Dirk. "The actual *New York Times*?"

"Yes sir, Mr. Bragg!" said the manager. "Listen," he said, reaching into his jacket pocket, "I don't mean to be a bother, but my wife is a huge fan." He produced a CD and a pen. "Would you mind?"

"Oh, not at all!" exclaimed Dirk. He grabbed the CD and scrawled his name. "Listen, Marge," he said, handing back the CD. "You sure I don't need to clean up a bit? I know I'm not usually a paragon of fashion or cleanliness, but—"

He motioned at himself. He was still as wild, dirty, and unkempt as he was when they found him in the woods.

"You look perfect, Dirk," said Marge. "Authentic wild-man. They'll love it. Wilderness chic."

Dirk dusted himself off. It made not a whiff of difference to how dirty he was. "If you say so, Marge," he said. "Well, let's not keep them waiting any longer."

The manager led them through a set of doors. Dozens of cameras flashed as they looked out at a sea of camera lenses, phones, and reporters. Dirk and Marge took seats at a table behind a pair of microphones.

"All right," said Marge, leaning into her mic. "Thank you for coming, everyone. My name is," she began, glancing at Dirk, "Diamond Marge, from Diamond Marge Management. I know none of you came to hear from me, so I'll not waste any more of your time. Mr. Bragg will give a brief statement and take a few questions."

The cameras began to flash again as the photographers sought to document Dirk's first public statement in many months. He cleared his throat.

"Um, yes," he said. "Thank you, Diamond Marge." He drew out a crumpled piece of paper, laid it on the table, and smoothed it out with his palms. "I just wanted to say I'm sorry, I guess, for taking off like I did. I know a lot of people were worried about me. I appreciated all the concern. I just...needed to..." He glanced at Marge. She gave him an encouraging smile. "I just needed to take a break from the spotlight. I'm just a reporter. I'm not used to being the story. And, uh, yeah. I guess that's it."

Shutters clicked. Every reporter in the room called his name, hoping to be picked first to ask a question.

"Yes, you with the hat," said Marge, pointing at a reporter in the front row.

"Yes, thank you," said the woman. "Mr. Bragg, I guess the question on everyone's mind is: where did you go?"

Dirk looked from Marge to the reporter. "The woods," he said simply.

Cameras flashed. Reporters wrote furiously in their notebooks.

"Next question," said Marge, pointing at another reporter.

"Dirk, there are some who say this comeback concert has the makings of the biggest musical spectacle since the turn of the century, with more than a hundred thousand concertgoers and a potential television audience in the millions. How does that make you feel?"

Dirk leaned towards his microphone. "Nice," he said. "It feels…nice."

More flashes. Reporters jostled to get his attention.

"Yes, you in the back?" said Marge, pointing.

"Thank you," he said. "Dirk, your disappearance was met with conspiracy theory after conspiracy theory—many of them connected to stories you had recently published in the *Really Real News* about the existence of werewolves. I have a two-part question: do you believe in werewolves, and did your disappearance have anything to do with them?"

Dirk cleared his throat. This was the question he had been dreading. He and Marge had drilled his response during the drive to the conference centre.

All of his life, Dirk had strived to reveal the truth about werewolves. At this moment, he had to bury that compulsion as deep as possible.

"No," he said robotically. "I do...not...believe in werewolves."

Dozens of people gasped. Reporters shouted follow-up questions.

"And I took some time off to get out of the spotlight," said Dirk. "Anything that suggests it had to do with anything supernatural is—" he closed his eyes "—nonsense."

Dirk was drowned out by the sound of every reporter in the room shouting more questions.

CHAPTER THIRTY-ONE

DR. BECK CLICKED THE LOCK BUTTON ON HER keys. She crossed the darkening parking lot of the building that housed her lab. As she climbed the short flight of steps, two men in black suits emerged from the front doors. One held the door open for her to enter.

"Thank you," she said.

He smiled. "Not a problem."

"Enjoy your evening, Dr. Beck," said the second man.

She blinked twice and thanked them again before the door shut behind her. She gave her head a little shake. She didn't recognize either of the men, but then again, several small start-up companies had labs in this building. She wasn't terribly good at remembering names and faces.

She hit the button to call the elevator to the first floor. The doors opened with a *ding*, and she stepped on.

She grinned as the elevator moved upward. It had been a fabulous day.

She'd worked late every night for the last week on Kate's problem. Despite her promises of a cure, her early attempts had not gone well. She could create the molecule she needed, one that flipped the protein switch to turn off the werewolf gene. The problem was, she couldn't make it stable. It would exist for a moment and dissolve into its base components.

But last night, *eureka*! In a moment borne out of frustration and failure, Dr. Beck threw part of her scientific brain out the window. If this cure had worked for Kate and her friends when they'd just stewed it on their kitchen stove, surely she could replicate it in the lab. She started mixing some of the raw ingredients to see what she would find.

That's when it happened.

Kronos's blood—the old-fashioned name for the sap of a cedar tree. She had been using a fairly sterile sample of the cure's active ingredient. But when she used actual syrup, straight from the jar she bought at the health-food store, it was like a light went on. Whatever was in that syrup stabilized the entire molecule. She would have to take some time to study exactly what was happening chemically to make it so stable, but for now, it worked.

She worked all day synthesizing the compound. By late afternoon, a few millilitres of the cure sat in the bottom of a test tube. It would have to be enough.

Dr. Beck packaged the cure in a travel-safe container and took it to the post office. She addressed it to Kate in New Brunswick and paid for the fastest delivery possible. That concert was in two days. She even bought insurance.

The elevator doors opened at her floor. She fished her keys from her bag and approached the door to her lab. She knew she should go home and get some sleep, but she couldn't. She couldn't let go of the idea that if she could make a cure, she could do the opposite. She could make herself into a werewolf—just like her grandfather. The answer was in the data. She just had to find it.

The logo for HappyGene Incorporated greeted her on the door to her lab. She reached out to insert her key in the lock.

"What the...."

The door was already unlocked and slightly open. She peeked through the crack. No one was inside. She pushed open the door and gasped.

The entire lab was in chaos. Broken glassware littered the countertops and floors. The testing array she used for genetic sequencing lay smashed on the ground. Papers were scattered everywhere. A crumpled piece of metal and plastic on her desk was all that was left of her laptop.

"My data!"

She turned over the laptop and found the hard drive had been carefully removed. She yanked open her desk drawer where she kept the external drive with her back-up data. It was gone.

Gone.

Everything she needed to synthesize the cure was gone. All the data she needed to begin work on becoming a wolf herself was lost. Brewing this cure wasn't as simple as mixing the ingredients of an old recipe. It would take months to rebuild what was taken.

She ran to the window. A blue car was pulling out of the parking lot. Inside were the two men she'd seen at the entrance to the building. She couldn't make out their license plate.

Twenty minutes on the phone with the police was enough to let her know they wouldn't be much help. The guard in the lobby hadn't seen a thing—he had been too busy trying to figure out why all the surveillance cameras in the building had suddenly gone blank. The police promised to send an officer to help her catalogue her stolen and broken equipment, but the chances of actually catching the men were slim to none.

Tears welled up in her eyes as she hung up. She pulled up her contacts and searched for Kate's number.

"Dr. Beck, is that you?" answered Kate.

"It's me," Dr. Beck said, forcing herself to smile. "Kate, I've got some good news and some bad news."

CHAPTER THIRTY-TWO

"BUT YOU PROMISED IT WOULD BE SAFE!" SAID Kate's mum over the phone. "You said it would be a nice quiet visit to the cabin!"

"Yeah, well, things kinda changed," said Kate with a wince. "A bit."

Kate had the cellphone to one ear and a finger in the other. Her mum had called at the worst time. Kate was waving in and out of a throng of people backstage at Dirk's concert site. Roadies shoved past her with crates of gear.

"Changed a bit!" repeated her mother. "Kate, this is the furthest you could possibly be from 'a nice quiet visit!' You're putting on a mega concert for thousands of people!"

"Oh, Mum," said Kate. "I'm so sorry. When Marcus got caught, we couldn't exactly leave him."

Lisa sighed. "I know," she said. "It's just, I worry about you and your brother."

"Mum, we'll be fine. We've planned it all out."

"You make sure you are," said Lisa. "I know I can trust you. You've always been so capable."

Kate heard her father shout in the background. "She gets that from me, you know."

Kate blushed. "Listen, Mum. I gotta go. I promise, things will be fine. We're going to take care of all of this."

"Okay, sweetie," said Lisa. "Take care. And watch out for your brother."

"I will," said Kate. "Bye."

Kate slid her phone into her pocket and looked around.

"Now, where is everyone?" she said to herself.

"My wheels belong to the road," sang Dirk's voice from a nearby tent.

"But my heaaaartt...belongs to yooouuu!" chimed in the members of his band in perfect country harmony.

Kate peeked in. Dirk strummed a guitar. His band stood behind him.

The fiddle player took two steps forward to play a sweet solo that made Kate think about country roads and pickup trucks. A woman with a pair of braids down her back plucked at a double bass. A man in a poor-boy hat scrawled away at a banjo. Kate had to admit: the band Dirk's record label had assembled to accompany him for this concert was pretty terrific, even if she didn't much care for country music.

The band had arrived just one day before the concert and they needed to squeeze in as much practice time as they could before the show. This tent was just a few dozen metres behind the giant stage currently being erected by a crew of workers.

The band strummed their final note and put down their instruments.

"Hey, that's coming along!" said the bass player.

"That fiddle solo was perfect," said the banjo player.

"Awesome work, everyone," agreed Dirk. "I think this is going to be terrific. Let's leave it there for now. Go grab supper."

"Thanks, Dirk!"

"Sure thing, boss."

The band chatted and laughed as they packed their gear and walked out. Dirk was locking his guitar into its case when Kate approached.

"That really sounded great," she said. "I guess you're not entirely without talent."

Dirk smiled. "Aw, go on," he said dryly. "You're going to give me a swelled head."

"No, I mean it," said Kate. "I think you're going to knock 'em dead."

Dirk paused. "That's nice of you, Kate. Thank you."

"You definitely kept up your end of the bargain," said Kate. "And more. I never realized what a big deal this would become. So, here."

She thrust a small vial toward him.

Dirk looked at it. "Is that what I think it is?"

"It is," said Kate. "The Cure."

He reached out slowly and took it. "Wow," he said. "And they say the solution to life's problems isn't found in a bottle."

"I think they're talking about something else in your case, Dirk."

"Maybe."

"Listen," said Kate. "I'm sure when this whole concert thing is over, you're going to be whisked off on some private jet to start your new life as a celebrity. So, if I don't see you again, I just wanted to say thanks."

"You're welcome, Kate," said Dirk.

"And you got what you wanted," said Kate. "You don't have to be a—what did you call it? A 'dirty, disgusting, no-good werewolf' anymore."

Dirk winced. "Did I say that?"

"Word for word."

"Ouch," said Dirk. "Okay, well, I guess I'm big enough to admit when I've been wrong. It's been kind of fun the last couple of weeks. You and your family, you're...you're all pretty nice people."

"We're nice ducks and wolves, too."

Dirk smiled. "Yes, you are." He offered his hand. "Katie Wereduck, it's been a pleasure working with you."

She grabbed his hand and gave it a shake. "You, too," she said. "Dirt Bag."

"Do people really call me that?"

"All the time," said Kate. "Oh, hey," she continued. "One last thing about that cure. So, like, you heard the story about Dr. Beck's lab. It's the only cure we have, and the only cure we're likely to have for a long time. So we can't waste it."

"Got it."

"But more importantly, it's most effective if you take it right before the call of the moon. That's the moment the genetic switch flips from human to were-wolf. Take it as close as you can to the moment before the sun goes down. Okay?"

"I got it," he said. "I promise."

"Okay, well, I've got to meet John over by the jail. Take care of yourself, Dirk."

"You, too," said Dirk. "Gosh, I feel like I should give you something. I wish I'd thought of this earlier—wait!"

He rummaged in a bag behind him and withdrew a banana. It was bright yellow with a touch of green at the end.

"Here," he said, handing it over. "It's my last one."

Kate thought she might cry.

CHAPTER THIRTY-THREE

"TESTING, ONE TWO. TESTING, ONE TWO," SAID Jolene. She adjusted the headset mic she was wearing and looked at her brother in the back of the van. "Thunk, you hearing me okay?"

He gave her a thumbs-up.

"Awesome," she said. "And the wireless is working? I want to be able to walk around freely in the concert area."

He nodded.

"Okay," said Jolene. "We're ready to roll."

"I still can't believe this is where you guys broadcast D-Net," said Bobby, his eyes darting around the back of Thunk's van. "This makes my old ham radio look like it was made in the Stone Age."

"Hey, man. Don't you dare knock the RF-Master 2000," said Jolene. "That is a classic piece of amateur radio technology."

"Right," said Bobby. "Sorry."

"But yeah, this stuff is pretty wicked," said Jolene, giving him a playful elbow to the ribs. "Thunk's got the whole rig tricked out pretty sweet. Look at this: it's a rolling frequency generator, secure real-time encryption, and an FX rack that can make you sound like Darth Vader."

"Cool," said Bobby.

"Yeah."

"So you've worked out a code with the D-Net hackers?"

"Yup. The whole network has been amazing with this whole thing. They were able to get me access to everything. Blueprints of the prison. Prisoner manifest. Guard rotation schedule. I've got the whole thing timed out perfectly."

"How's it going to work?"

"Come here, I'll show you."

Bobby hopped into the van beside Jolene as she tapped a few keys on her laptop.

"So Marcus is locked up in cellblock D," she said, pointing to a section of the prison blueprints on her screen. "All we really need to know about that is there are four locked doors between him and freedom. One for his cell. One for the cellblock. One for the back door—he's going out through the guard's smoking exit—and one for the fence. They're all controlled by electronic locks."

"Right," said Bobby.

"There's a shift change with the guards about twenty minutes before sundown," Jolene explained. "That's our best window for him to escape. The evening guards like to yack in the lunchroom over coffee for about ten minutes before their first walkthrough."

"You were able to find that out from D-Net?"

"Oh man, it's awesome," said Jolene, shutting her laptop. "Someone mentioned it in the minutes for a meeting of the guard's union about two months ago. God bless the internet."

"Okay, so how do you signal D-Net to unlock the doors?"

"We can't do all four at once," said Jolene. "It'd be way too suspicious. I've got a code for each door that I'll say when I'm doing my broadcast from the concert. Each door will be unlocked for ten seconds. That should be time enough for Marcus to squeeze out."

"That's cutting it pretty close," said Bobby.

Jolene nodded and shrugged. "I mean, it's that, or some guard stumbles across an unlocked door and sounds the alarm," said Jolene. "It's going to work. I know it. Marcus can handle it."

"I hope so," said Bobby.

Jolene hopped out of the van. She wore an all-access pass to the concert around her neck. The parking lot was already packed with cars. There were license plates from every province in Canada and most states of the US.

"Dirk really is a big deal, eh?" said Bobby.

"Yeah. That's why this is going to work." She looked at her phone. "Concert is about to begin. Let's do this."

CHAPTER THIRTY-FOUR

THE CHANTING WAS GETTING LOUDER. DIRK HID behind a curtain at the edge of the giant stage. He knew there would be a lot of people, but a crowd of a hundred thousand people is a much different thing in real life. And almost every person was chanting his name.

"Five minutes to showtime, boss," said a voice behind him. It was Gerry, the banjo player. "I been in a lot of big shows before, but this crowd takes the cake. This is gonna be one for the books."

"I guess so," said Dirk.

"I gotta say," continued Gerry, "I was pretty nervous when they asked me to come up here to play with you. I mean, I read the stories. There were loads of people saying some pretty Looney Tunes things about you."

"Uh huh," said Dirk.

"I mean, werewolves?" said Gerry with a chuckle. "That's crazy talk. And a couple of the stories said you thought there was such a crazy thing as a were*duck*." Gerry shook his head. "I told myself before I came up here that if you started talking about weird stuff like that, I'd quit right away. But you're all right, Bragg. This is gonna be just fine." He patted Dirk on the back and walked away.

Dirk thought about the vial in his pocket. Just one drink and all his problems would melt away. He wouldn't be Dirk the werewolf. He wouldn't even be Dirk the reporter. He'd be Dirk the country music star.

It had been all he'd dreamed about for months as he stewed in that cabin in the woods. His music had become famous all over the world while he languished in a forest in some godforsaken corner of Canada. All because he believed he had become something awful. Something terrible.

He had searched for werewolves his entire adult life. It was just part of who he was. He had gone to work at *Really Real News* because he wanted to prove these terrifying creatures were real. He wanted to find the truth and be the first to tell the world. But where had that fascination with werewolves begun? Why werewolves?

It came to him in a flash: a book. A book with a black cover and yellow writing. *Enter the Lycanthrope*. He had found the book in the library when he was a kid. The image of the werewolf on the cover was burned into his memory. He remembered standing in front of the bookshelves with the book in hand, staring at that image. It was...terrifying. He didn't know why he wanted to take that book home, but he did.

He read it cover to cover.

The illustration was carefully rendered to not reveal very much at all. What you saw was the mere suggestion of claws, teeth, and eyes. The cover of that book was scary because of what it *didn't* show. Our fears flourish in the dark. And the picture of werewolves in his mind had recently been flooded with light. He could now see them for what they really were.

He wasn't afraid of werewolves now. They were his friends.

Dirk didn't have a lot of friends. He didn't have any, come to think of it. Tonight, after the show, his record label would whisk him off to God-knew-where. There was talk of recording studios, late-night talk show appearances, and tours. But would there be friends?

"Dirk! Dirk! Dirk! Dirk!" chanted the crowd.

"It's time, boss," said Gerry, reappearing and putting a hand on his shoulder. "Let's give 'em a show they'll never forget, eh?"

Dirk swallowed hard. "Okay."

They paused for a moment to listen to the chanting.

"Gosh, they love you," said Gerry.

"Yeah," said Dirk. He forced a smile. "Yeah, I think you're right."

CHAPTER THIRTY-FIVE

A LOW HUM RUMBLED FROM THE SPEAKERS IN Bobby's headphones. It sustained a low-frequency note for several seconds before slowly becoming higher. It finally reached a tone so high it was painful. He yanked his headphones off, waited a moment, and put them back on in time to hear the familiar, digitally altered voice.

"That should make sure none of the *freaks* are listening," said the voice. "You're listening to D-Net. We are your first and last authority on all things werewolf, were*duck*, and on the continuing search for the only man brave enough to speak truth to power. A man so dangerous to the status quo, the status quo stole him from us. I'm talking about Dirk Bragg."

Jolene strolled through the crowd at the concert site. She adjusted her headset so it rested more comfortably over hear ears. Dirk's concert had drawn an eclectic crowd, so she didn't stick out too much walking around with a microphone strapped to her head.

"We are broadcasting to you live from the concert of the century. That's right, D-Net: your old pal Shadow managed to secure himself a ticket to the Dirk Bragg concert." She glanced at her watch. "It's expected to start any minute, so don't go anywhere. In the meantime, let's talk conspiracy, shall we?"

Bobby, listening on a portable radio near the stage got a little flutter in his tummy. He'd forgotten how fun it was listening to D-Net.

"More than a year ago, Dirk Bragg published a series of stories about the existence of werewolves," said Jolene as Shadow. "He even revealed, for the first time, the existence of a creature previously unknown to anyone—a were*duck*. Shortly after the publication of these stories, Dirk mysteriously vanished.

"Now, we all tuned into the press conference a few days ago," continued Shadow, "where Dirk claimed he was simply taking a break from the limelight. He said fame had become too much for him to bear. He went on to deny he ever believed in werewolves." Shadow scoffed. "Friends, listeners, members of the D-Net collective—we know better, don't we?

"Would the man whose writings on the existence of werewolves we've loved for so many years suddenly change his tune?" asked Shadow. "I certainly don't think so. Not unless he had a reason.

"So let's think about what that reason might be. Maybe someone made him deny the truth. Maybe someone wore him down over the last nine months and broke his spirit. They're making him denounce the truth about werewolves in order to advance their own selfish goal—to sell more music. To make money. So maybe the music industry is to blame.

"Or maybe...that's not even Dirk at all? It might not be, dear listener. Perhaps it's a body double, sent to deceive us, while the real Dirk languishes in some unknown prison."

Jolene stopped walking and looked around. She was lost in a sea of thousands of people. She smiled. It was time to crank up the conspiracy a notch.

"Or maybe, just maybe, it's none of those things. What if Dirk Bragg has assembled the biggest audience he could muster—millions of people will be watching the telecast of this concert—so that he could blow their minds. What if Dirk Bragg is going to reveal the truth about werewolves to the world?" She paused for dramatic effect. "D-Net, that's what I think."

Jolene took another breath. Sometimes the best far-out theory was the one closest to the truth. She plowed on.

"I believe Dirk Bragg went into hiding because he *himself* has been turned into a werewolf. And he has come out of hiding on this night—this full moon night—to open all our eyes to the truth."

A hush fell on the crowd as the first bit of movement appeared on stage. Members of Dirk's band were taking their places and plugging into their amplifiers. The hush transformed into a giant cheer as the band began to play the first few bars of a slow country jam.

"Would you please put your hands together and welcome to the stage," boomed the voice of an announcer over the loudspeakers, "Mister! Dirk! Braaaagg!"

Thousands of voices cried out as Dirk emerged, an acoustic guitar strapped around his body. He stepped toward the microphone as the band continued to play.

"Thank you for coming, everyone."

The crowd went wild.

"I hope you enjoy some of my music," he said meekly, before turning to his band and strumming along.

"Dear listeners of D-Net," said Jolene/Shadow, "I believe Dirk will turn into a wolf tonight before our very eyes."

Marcus could hear the roar of the crowd from his cell. The prison was less than a kilometre away from the concert site. He could hear a shift in the sound as the band began to play.

He thought back to his visit from John and Jolene. She had told him to pay attention to everything on this night. He sat, listening carefully. Watching for anything unusual. He paid attention to absolutely everything, from the food he was served, to the movement of the guards. He was waiting for something, but for what, he had no idea.

CLUNK

The electronic lock on his cell door made a familiar sound. Marcus glanced down the hallway to see if the coast was clear. He pushed on the door. It swung opened easily.

CLUNK

The door locked itself again. That was close. If he hadn't opened the door in the few precious seconds it was unlocked, all would have been lost. He'd have to move quickly.

Marcus crept down the hall to the cellblock door. He crouched low below the window in the door and waited.

CHAPTER THIRTY-SIX

"THAT WAS THE SIGNAL!" SAID JOHN. HE AND KATE were sharing a pair of earbuds attached to Bobby's portable shortwave radio. "Before our very eyes!"

The pair crouched in the underbrush of the forest behind the jail. They were about thirty metres from the gate where Marcus would eventually emerge, if all went according to plan.

Kate stroked Wacka's back. "Okay," she said. "That means they've just tripped the lock on Marcus's cell, and, hopefully, cut the motion detector and cameras in the hallway."

"What do you mean 'hopefully?'" said John.

"Hey, I'm just saying."

"Say it more optimistically," he said. "This has to work."

"I was talking to *Wacka*."

"The duck doesn't need to know everything."

"The duck is a valued member of this team." Kate petted Wacka furiously. "Yes, you are," she said. "I affirm your value, Wacka."

"Wacka," said Wacka, blinking.

"Honestly," said John, shaking his head. "Okay, how long before the next signal?"

"Not long," said Kate. "Couple minutes."

"And what's the line for that one?"

"'You heard it here first, folks.'"

"And that's what we call the newsroom blue-oooooos!" sang Dirk from the stage. He turned to his band as they played the last three chords.

Dirk blushed as the crowd erupted in cheers. Their first number had gone perfectly.

"Thank you," he said softly into the microphone to another giant swell of cheers. "This next song is about, well, it's about bananas."

The crowd screamed.

"I really like bananas," added Dirk.

The band broke into the opening notes of "Perfect Banana" as he stepped back up to the mic.

"Yellow! I just called to say 'yellow,' and to ask, if you've got time for this fellow."

The song went on to describe the perfect banana— yellow with just a touch of green at the end, and not a spot of bruising.

"For a perr-fect banana there's not much I wouldn't do!
Just one tiny taste, and I'll never be blue!
But if I had a perfect banana there's one thing I know is true.
If I had a perfect banana—I'd like to share it with you.
Yes, if I had a perfect banana, I'd share it with you."

Thousands of people screamed in adoration. Dirk was flabbergasted. This crowd really seemed to love him.

This would be his life now. Mega concerts. Millions of fans. Leaving that crazy family of werewolves behind him. It was what he wanted. Wasn't it? Just now, he wasn't so sure. As Dirk sang a song about sharing a banana with a friend, he felt perfectly alone.

"Our boy Dirk really is going for it," said Jolene into her headset. "Dirk Bragg, a man who has dug deeper into the conspiracy of werewolves than anyone before him, is singing an earnest song about the love of an unblemished banana."

Jolene paused a moment to let that last bit sink in. She was making up nonsense on the spot to distract whoever Project Firefly was, but it had to be said. This concert was weird. She looked at her watch. It was time for the next signal.

"The love of a banana," she repeated. "You heard it here first, folks."

CLUNK

Marcus turned the handle of the cellblock door and pulled. He peered down the next hallway. The coast was clear. He could go right or left.

There's no way they'd send me toward the guard's break room, thought Marcus.

He dashed left. At the end of the corridor was a door marked *Emergency Exit*. Beside it was taped a piece of paper on which someone had written: *Please place your cigarette butts in the receptacle provided.*

This had to be it. Marcus crouched and waited.

CHAPTER THIRTY-SEVEN

KATE LOOKED AT THE SKY. THE SUN WAS GETTING awfully low. "Why do we always have to cut this stuff so close?" she said.

"This was your plan, remember?" said John.

"I know, but still."

"Look, he's already gone through two doors," said John. "That's halfway! He's on the other side of that emergency exit right now. He just has to make it through there and through the gate at the fence."

"And it's how long until sunset?"

John looked at his watch.

"Thirteen minutes."

"Thirteen," she repeated. "So lucky."

"The next cue must be coming up," said John. "What's the line we're waiting for?"

"'That's the way the cookie crumbles.'"

Kate and John put their earbuds back in.

Jolene was running out of things to talk about.

"Conspiracy is an interesting word," said Jolene as Shadow. "The dictionary tells us it's a noun meaning 'a secret plan by a group to do something unlawful or harmful.' Track the word through history, and you'll find it didn't always have a negative connotation. Even the word 'conspire' doesn't always mean you have ill intent. Go back far enough to the Latin origin and it simply means 'an agreement.'"

She was really reaching now. She looked at her phone. She had to riff for another minute before she was scheduled to give the next cue.

On stage, Dirk was wrapping up another song. This one was about the lack of respect a tabloid journalist typically receives.

"Thank you," said Dirk in response to the hearty cheer. "I wish I had enough of my own songs to play for you for hours and hours, but I don't. So I'm going to play a few songs from artists I admire. This next one is by the great Dolly Parton.

Jolene cringed. She knew what was coming. It was a song she had loathed for as long as she could remember.

"Jolene, Jolene, Jolene, Joleeeene!" sang Dirk.

"Oh, my God, dear D-Net," said Jolene as Shadow. "He's singing the classic hits now. Many people love this song very, very much," she said. "This is may be more personal information than you would normally expect from your humble host, but my very own parents love this song." She glared at Dirk on stage. "A lot."

She looked at her phone.

"I, myself, am not a huge fan of it. But here we are. That's the way the cookie crumbles."

CLUNK

Marcus turned the handle and walked through the door. He was outside. He passed a metal ashtray marked *BUTT STATION* and sprinted across the asphalt towards a gate in the fence.

"There he is!" said John. He stood up and waved an arm. "Dad! Over here!"

"Shhh!" hissed Kate, motioning for John to lie low. "We're not out of this yet. We've got one more lock to go."

"And what's the cue for that?" asked John, stuffing the earbud back in his ear.

"She's got to say 'that's all she wrote.'"

"Oh, my God, I hope she does this quick."

Marge peeked out into the crowd from her position backstage. She really couldn't believe the size of this audience. If the goal of the night had been to actually put on a mega concert, she'd be sipping champagne and toasting her success.

She spotted Bobby in the crowd. He had made his way to the front near the stage and was cheering with the best of them. And why not? These kids had been through so much. It was okay for him to enjoy himself for once.

About halfway into the sea of people, she caught a glimpse of Jolene. Her eyes were locked onto the stage. She was speaking a steady stream into her headset mic.

Good. Everything was going to plan.

A few metres behind Jolene stood two men who looked out of place. They wore black suits and ties. They were much more interested in watching Jolene than what was happening on stage.

"What on earth could that be about?" muttered Marge.

Thunk tapped away at a laptop in the back of the van. He wiped beads of sweat from his forehead. Whoever was tracing the signal he was broadcasting was awfully good. Every time he shifted frequencies, they shifted with him. He tried encrypting it in several different ways, but they always adjusted to compensate. It was only a matter of time before they would have a lock on his location.

He pushed a fader to bounce his signal from another tower. That might save him another minute or two. He was ready for whoever was tracking him to adjust again. He prepared a quick batch of code to start a brand new layer of encryption at the slightest indication of interference.

Seconds ticked by. The seconds became a minute. This was weird.

Whoever was trying to track the signal had suddenly stopped. There was no evidence of anyone trying to lock them down to a specific location. What had just a moment ago been a constant struggle for the signal seemed to be over. Maybe they'd given up?

A loud screeching filled his ears. He yanked off his headphones.

When he put them back on, there was nothing. Not a sound. He couldn't hear Jolene.

He tapped his keyboard. Nothing. Either the screen had burned out, or the whole computer was fried.

He turned to the console. Every light and display had gone out.

They had shut him down. He had no idea how they'd done it, but the D-Net broadcast was offline.

"Oh no," said Thunk.

CHAPTER THIRTY-EIGHT

JOLENE HAD NO IDEA SHE WAS OFF THE AIR. SHE was still talking into the microphone, delving deep in to the etymology of the word "werewolf." She looked at her phone. Just a minute left and she'd give the final cue to unlock the gate and set Marcus free.

"Jolene!" yelled a voice. "Jolene!"

Gosh, she hated that song. So many people loved it. Now some idiot was screaming for an encore performance.

"Jolene!" cried the voice. It was a boy. And his voice was vaguely familiar. She spun around.

Thunk was charging through the crowd. His face was red. He looked mortified.

"Jolene!" he yelled.

He pushed between two men in suits. Neither Jolene nor Thunk noticed the men smirk at each other before retreating into the crowd.

Jolene ripped off her headphones. "Thunk, what are you doing, man? Who is running the broadcast?"

His eyes bugged out. He drew his finger across his throat.

"Someone cut the signal?" she yelled.

He nodded.

"Who?"

He put his hands on his hips as if to say the answer was obvious.

"Right," she said. "Firefly."

Thunk tapped his watch.

"Oh, my gosh. You're right," said Jolene. "How are we going to give the next signal?"

Thunk shrugged.

"Oh, you're a huge help."

Thunk frowned.

"I'm sorry." She touched his arm. "I know it's not your fault."

Thunk smiled.

"So what do we do next?"

"Bob," Thunk said. "Marge."

"Yeah, you're right," said Jolene. "Let's go!"

Bobby stood at the front of the stage, sipping a bottle of water. Dirk and his band had just finished the first set and were backstage for intermission.

Bobby had originally been ticked off he didn't have a real job in this rescue plan, but after a few songs, he started to get really into the concert. He even met some cool guys who taught him how to crowd surf. He looked around to see if any of his new pals were still nearby. Instead he saw Jolene and Thunk pushing their way through the crowd.

"Oh hey, guys," he said cheerfully. "What's up? Awesome concert, eh?"

"Bobby, this is horrible," said Jolene. "We're off the air."

"Off the air?" repeated Bobby. "That's horrible!" His face screwed up in confusion. "Wait, why is that horrible?"

"Because if I can't give the signal to unlock the last gate, nobody will unlock the last gate!"

"Oh, dang!" said Bobby, thinking quickly. "Okay, let's go see Dirk and Grandma."

"What're they going to do?" said Jolene.

"I dunno," said Bobby with a shrug. "But telling them is better than just sitting here."

"They're off the air," said John. "Kate, they're off the air. D-Net is off the air!"

"John, I can *hear*," said Kate, removing her earbud.

"But we're screwed!" said John. "Screwed!"

"Okay, let's calm down and think," said Kate.

They looked at each other. They looked at Marcus. He was so exposed, standing out in the open by the fence gate. If he stayed there much longer, he'd be spotted for sure.

"Okay, thinking sucks," said Kate. "Let's go see your dad."

They ran through the underbrush and emerged at the edge of the forest. Marcus' eyes lit up when he saw them.

"John!" he called. "Kate!"

"Dad!"

"I'm so glad you're here!" Marcus said. "I don't know how you guys did all this, but it's amazing. Just unlock this gate, and I'm out of here."

"Yeah, about that, Dad," said John awkwardly. "I don't know how to open this."

"The broadcast is *what*?" said Dirk and Marge together.

"Off the air," said Jolene. "Dead. Done. Nothing. There is no broadcast."

"And Marcus is still in jail?" said Dirk.

"Yes," said Bobby.

"And we have no way to unlock that final gate?" said Marge.

"That's it," said Jolene.

Dirk thought for a minute. "How long until sundown?" he said.

Jolene looked at her phone. "Eight minutes."

Dirk paused a moment. He knew exactly what he needed to do. "Gerry," he called to his banjo player.

"Yeah, boss?"

"Gerry, I've got a bit of a bathroom problem. I know we have to go back on stage in a few minutes, but can you stall for me?"

"No prob, boss," he said with a wink and a pat of his tummy. "Happens to the best of us."

"What's going on?" asked Marge.

Dirk spun to face her. "Diamond Marge," he said. "You're the best manager I've ever had."

Marge made a face.

"Marge, I gotta take off," said Dirk. "My little bathroom break will only buy us a few minutes. I need a whole lot more minutes than that."

"What are you doing?" she asked.

"No time to explain," he said. "Just...stall."

"Stall who?"

Dirk pointed towards the stage and the thousands of screaming fans.

"Them," he said. He turned to Bobby, Thunk, and Jolene. "The rest of you, come with me."

"I hope you know what you're doing!" called Marge.

"Trust me!" he shouted over his shoulder.

Marge narrowed her eyes. "Dirt Bag," she muttered.

Dirk rushed through the dressing area and grabbed an oversized orange jacket.

"Can I have this?" called Dirk to a member of the stage crew.

"You're Dirk," said the man. "You can have anything."

"Thanks!" yelled Dirk, running out of the dressing area.

Bobby, Thunk, and Jolene struggled to keep up as Dirk darted through backstage tents.

"What's happening?" called Jolene.

"Just keep up!" called Dirk.

They lifted a flap and found themselves outside at the back of the sea of tents. Dirk pulled on the jacket and positioned the hood so it covered most of his face.

"Now what?" said Bobby.

They stood beside a small fleet of golf carts for the production staff.

"Can any of you drive?" said Dirk.

"Thunk can. Why?" said Jolene.

"Can you drive a golf cart?" Dirk asked Thunk.

Thunk's eyes darted from Dirk to Jolene and back to Dirk. He nodded.

"Good," he said, hopping into the passenger seat of the nearest cart. "Hop in. We don't have much time to lose."

"Ready in two," said the stage manager into his headset. "Randy, what can we do about that spotlight on stage left? The bass player says it nearly blinded her in the first half of the show." He listened for a moment. "Mm-hmm. Mm-hmm. Okay, just make it happen."

He looked up and found Marge standing in front of him.

"Diamond Marge!" the stage manager said. "First half was terrific. Your boy really can bring it. Now, where is he? I need to talk to him about the second—"

"About that," interrupted Marge. She put a hand on his shoulder and began to walk him toward the stage. "Dirk and I honestly weren't as thrilled with the first half as you were. We've got some changes we'd like to make before he comes back on stage."

The stage manager ripped off his headset. "Changes?" he sputtered. "But the show restarts in literally *one* minute."

"Oh, well then," said Marge. She slid on her sunglasses. "Guess you'll have to work quickly, won't you?"

CHAPTER THIRTY-NINE

"CAREFUL. EXCUSE US. PARDON US. SORRY," SAID Bobby as the golf cart wove its way through the crowds.

"Can't this thing go any faster?" said Dirk.

Thunk looked terrified and shook his head.

Dirk looked at his watch. "Six minutes until sunset."

"Someone is going to recognize you," said Jolene. "The cart is going to be swamped by fans and we'll be totally out of luck."

Dirk pulled the hood lower over his face. He glanced around and saw an opening in the crowd.

"No time to explain!" he yelled at Thunk as he grabbed the wheel and steered it hard to the right.

"Whoooooaaa!" yelled Jolene and Bobby as they struggled to stay in their seats.

"There, right through there," said Dirk, pointing.

There were headed for a spot at the edge of the

concert site. The only people in the area were two police officers securing the concert's perimeter.

"Okay, this had better work," said Dirk.

One of the officers put his hand up to stop them. "Whoa, whoa, whoa," he said. "What's the hurry this evening, friends?"

Dirk pulled off his hood. "Good evening, officers," he said. "I hope you're having a good time."

"Dirk Bragg!" gasped one of the cops.

"I can't believe it's you!" said the other.

"Fellas, I'm going to cut to the chase: I need to get out of this concert site for a few moments to get some fresh air," said Dirk. "Mind if I just give you both autographs and you let us through, no questions asked?"

The first officer looked at the other.

"Well," said the first.

"I dunno," said the second.

They burst out laughing.

"Of course you can, Mr. Bragg," said the first officer. He fished a small notebook from his pocket. "Can you sign mine 'to my good friend Mike Anderson?'"

"And mine 'to my best bud Dan Dufour?'"

"Anything for fans," said Dirk, scribbling his name as quickly as he could.

"Dad, I'm so sorry," said John. "We've let you down."

"No, no. Don't apologize," said Marcus through the fence. "I mean, it had to come out eventually. It will be hard, but maybe people will surprise us. Maybe werewolves and humans can actually live together."

"You really think that?" said Kate.

Marcus sighed. "Not really," he said. "But it sounded nice. And it made me feel better for a minute."

"Sorry," said Kate.

John looked at the horizon. "Sun's almost gone, Dad. Another minute or two."

"Yeah," he said. "Another minute or two of peace."

"I'm so sorry, Dad."

"Please," said Marcus. "No more apologies. You're sorry. I'm sorry. Kate's sorry. Let's just...be with each other for one last minute. One last minute of quiet."

Kate closed her eyes. They'd worked so hard to set Marcus free. They'd come *so* close but they'd failed. She wiped away the tears forming in her eyes with the back of her hand.

No one spoke. All was quiet but for the faint sound of the concert crowd chanting for Dirk. It had been swelling in the background for a few minutes. It was now loud enough she could make out the words.

"Bring back Dirk! Bring back Dirk! Bring back Dirk!"

Bring back Dirk? thought Kate. *He should be on stage, a couple songs into his second set by now.*

Another sound broke her train of thought. Something Kate couldn't put her finger on. It sounded like...screaming? And it was getting closer.

Suddenly, a golf cart crashed through the trees. Branches and twigs went flying as the cart barrelled towards them.

"Whooooooooaaaa!" screamed the passengers.

The cart plowed over the long grass and weeds at the edge of the forest and screeched to a halt beside the gate. Bobby spilled onto the ground. He lay face down, hugging the earth.

"I'm never...driving...anywhere...ever again," he said.

Thunk and Jolene sat frozen and wide-eyed in their seats, traumatized by the ride.

"Oh, hi again," said Dirk, popping up as if nothing was amiss. He pulled the hood back from his face and strode toward the gate. "I understand you're having some trouble."

"Dirk?" said Kate. "You're supposed to be—"

"On stage?" said Dirk. "Legions of adoring fans, chanting my name? Yes, your grandmother is taking care of all that for me."

Kate looked blankly. "What?"

"Sorry, no time to explain. I hear Marcus is in a bit of a pickle."

"You could say that, Dirt Bag," growled Marcus.

"Oh, yes," said Dirk. "I'd forgotten you kind of hate me."

"Double-crossing and revenge tend to breed ill feelings," said Marcus.

"Oh, well I'm terribly sorry," said Dirk. "But I do have something that might help."

"Something to unlock this door?"

Dirk frowned. "Nothing like that, I'm afraid." He dug into his pants pocket and pulled out a vial. "I do have *this*, however."

Marcus looked at him. "What's that?"

"It's the cure," said Kate with wide eyes. "It's the Cure for Werewolf."

"And what am I supposed to do with that?" asked Marcus. "How's that going to unlock the door?"

"It won't, frankly," said Dirk. "But John tells me the hands of justice have offered you some sort of plea bargain."

"What does that have to do with anything?" said Marcus, now even more confused.

"Do I have to spell it out?" said Dirk. "Drink this, and you'll be a free man in a month. You won't be a werewolf, but you'll be free."

Marcus stared at him through the fence.

"Dad, he's right," said John. "Take it."

"Why would you give this to me?" demanded Marcus.

"Dirk, it's yours, remember?" said Kate. "That was the deal. You held up your part of the bargain. It's the only Cure for Werewolf we're likely to have for years."

"I know," said Dirk. "But if it's mine, it's mine to do with what I please. And what I please is to help my friends."

Everyone stared at him.

"I'm talking about all of you," said Dirk.

"But the concert," said Kate.

"I mean, it was fun, but I really can't finish if I'm a werewolf, can I? It's terribly hard to strum the guitar with paws."

He mimed playing a guitar with closed fists.

"But your career!" insisted Kate. "You're going to be a mega star."

Dirk shrugged. "Fame isn't everything."

Jolene butted in. "Look, all this touchy-feely stuff is amazing, but whatever is going to happen better happen quick." She pointed at the sun. "Look."

The sky around it was ablaze in orange and pink. It would set in seconds.

Dirk held out the vial. "Take it."

Marcus held his gaze for a second longer and grabbed the vial. He unscrewed the cap and drank its contents. He winced.

"Feel anything?" John wanted to know.

"Feels...warm," Marcus said, replacing the cap. He wiped his mouth with the back of his hand.

"And?" asked Kate.

"And, a bit...I don't know."

He doubled over and clutched his stomach.

"Marcus!"

"Dad!"

Marcus hit the ground in a heap, still grabbing his gut. "What's happening?" he gasped.

Kate watched helplessly from the other side of the fence. There was nothing she could do.

"Oh, Dad," said John. He grabbed the fence.

"Oh, God," grunted Marcus, rolling back and forth. "This is...this is...."

All of a sudden he sat straight up. "Over," he said between breaths. "It's over."

"What?" said Kate, as Marcus stood up and dusted himself off.

"It's the weirdest thing," he said. "I feel completely normal. It's like nothing happened. Like, one second I was...."

Marcus kept talking as another familiar voice began to call. Kate looked west and saw the sun had just set.

"Whoooooooo?" called the moon.

Marcus kept talking.

"Marcus," interrupted Kate. "Don't you hear it?"

Marcus looked from Kate to John and, finally, to Dirk. He smiled.

"Hear what?"

"It worked!" said Dirk.

"Oh, my gosh, Dad," said John.

Marcus smiled at them all. He put his fist against the fence. "Thanks, Dirk."

"You're welcome," said Dirk, placing his fist against Marcus's. "Kind of crazy that from here on out, you'll be the normal guy and I'll be the weirdo."

"Dirk," said John. "You were always the weirdo."

Dirk laughed. "I supposed you're right," he said. He shrugged before throwing back his head to howl.

His body twisted and contorted as he began to change.

"Oh...my...*God*," whispered Jolene, her eyes wide. "It's really happening. I'm really watching this."

"Cool, right?" said Bobby.

"Cool," whispered Thunk.

Dirk the wolf stepped toward Kate and looked up at her. She touched his head, like she was about to pet him.

"You're being called, Kate," said Marcus. He winked. "You'd better answer."

"I will," she said, looking up. "And I'll see you in a few weeks, Marcus." She bumped his fist through the fence. "*Quack!*" she called.

Kate's clothes became baggy and loose around her as she began to shrink. Her fingers dissolved into a fine point as her skin sprouted feathers and a bill. In a moment, she was a mottled brown mallard standing on a pile of her clothes.

Jolene's eyes were huge. "This is *so wild*," she said, taking out her phone. "Wait until D-Net hears about this."

Thunk scowled at her.

"Aw, jeesh," she said, repocketing the phone. "Okay, okay, okay. You don't have to lecture me. I won't say anything."

Thunk smiled.

"KATIE!" called Wacka's human voice from the bushes. "KATIE, WACKA IS NAKED IN THE BUSHES."

Bobby picked up Kate's clothes.

"I'm closing my eyes so I don't see anything!" he said, walking blindly towards the woods, holding the clothes in front of him.

"WHY?" said Wacka. "BOBBEE MIGHT WALK INTO A—"

"*Oomph*!" said Bobby, as his head collided with a tree branch. "Okay, I'm just going to throw them."

He balled the clothes up and tossed them into the woods.

"THANK YOU, BOB-BEE!"

"You'd all better get out of here," said Marcus to John, Bobby, Jolene, and Thunk. "You don't want to be here when the guards show up."

"Think you'll be okay?" said John.

"Oh yeah," said Marcus. "I'll just say they forgot me out here when we had our exercise break earlier. The night guards already blame the day guards for everything anyway. They'd love to have something like this to pin on them."

"Okay," said John. "Take care, Dad. See you soon."

Marcus smiled. "I'll see you soon."

John paused. "Are you okay?" he said. "You're not a wolf anymore."

Marcus smiled. "Yeah, I'm okay." He shrugged slightly. "I know someone else who went through something similar. Maybe he can help."

John nodded. "I'm sure he can."

Marcus stood at the gate and watched as three boys, two girls, a wolf, and a duck disappeared into the forest.

CHAPTER FORTY

Six months later

KATE SAT BESIDE THE CAMPFIRE AND SIPPED A CUP of tea. She was playing a game with Wacka. Kate set down her tea and held up two balled fists.

"Which hand, Wacka? Where's the sunflower seed?"

Wacka waddled over and pecked at Kate's left hand.

"You are ridiculously good at this," said Kate, opening her left hand to reveal the seed. Wacka gobbled it up.

Kate sighed and looked around. Even though it had been half a year, she was still so glad to be home. It almost felt like they'd never left this little spot in the woods. When all the dust had settled after the big concert, her mum and dad decided it was safe enough to move back.

John lived close enough to visit on weekends. School was better for him now that he and Jolene had managed to establish a solid friendship. She was still more than capable of devilishly complicating any group homework they undertook, but she did it with a knowing smirk on her face.

Marge emerged from the woodpile behind the shed. She dropped an armload of wood beside the fire.

"Good morning, Kate my dear," she said. "Is there tea?"

"There's always tea, Grandma."

"That's a good girl," said Marge, as Kate filled her cup. "What time are John and company expected?"

"Sometime this morning. It'll be nice to see them."

"Even Thunk?" said Marge, trying hard to keep her voice even.

"What? We're just friends."

Marge blew on her tea and gave Kate a little wink.

"Grandma!"

"Hello, Marjorie!" called a voice from the edge of the clearing. Two men approached: one had dark hair and eyes; the other was a tangled mess of shaggy beard and brown hair.

"You know very well I hate being called that, Dirt Bag," replied Marge with dignity.

"Oh, but it's such a pretty name," chided Dirk, "for such a pretty lady."

"Stop flirting with the neighbours," said Marcus as he grabbed a mug.

To everyone's surprise, Marcus and Dirk had become friends. When the rest of Kate's family returned to their camp, Dirk and Marcus moved to the little abandoned house just up the road, where Dirk had made his hideout more than a year ago. Marcus was always saying he was about to take off, but he didn't seem to be in any rush.

"What, um, time did you say Jolene was arriving?" asked Dirk. He was trying to look cool and breezy. It wasn't working.

"Sometime this morning," said Kate, her eyes narrowed. "Why?"

"Oh, ha, no reason," said Dirk. "It'll just be nice to see her."

Marcus punched him in the arm.

"She's taping the interview with you today for D-Net, you dork," he said. "As if you didn't remember."

Dirk filled himself a mug of tea. "Oh, gosh, is that today?"

Everyone laughed.

"I mean, I have to give the fans what they want," he said with a shrug. "Six-month anniversary of my disappearance? Kind of fun to tease them a bit. Let them know I'm not dead."

"Who's dead?" said Bobby. He and his parents emerged from the cabin. Brian was still in his PJs.

"Dirk," said Marcus. He smirked. "It's a D-Net exclusive. His ghost came back to haunt us."

"Good lord, now we'll never be rid of him," said Lisa.

"That must be why he's always coming over looking for breakfast," said Brian.

"Can't a dead guy catch a break?" said Dirk.

Kate looked around the fire to the faces of her friends and family. She thought it again: it was good to be home.

"So, Bobby," said Dirk. "Big night, eh? Your first full moon. You ready for it, my man?"

Bobby jumped on a stump beside the fire. He crouched like a wolf and threw his head back in a mighty howl.

"That answers that," laughed Marcus.

"So you think you'll be a wolf?" said Kate. "You don't want to join Wacka and me on Team Duck?"

Bobby made a face. "Nah, I pretty much feel like a wolf, I think. That's how it works right?"

"Yup, that's how it works," said Kate.

"Unless…," said Bobby.

"Unless what?"

"I mean, wolves are fine and all," said Bobby. "But ever since I was little, I dunno. I just, kinda felt like it might be nice to be…a bear."

Kate's eyes went wide. "Bobby Werebear?"

Laughter drifted like smoke above the campfire.

EPILOGUE

DR. BECK FINISHED WIPING THE COUNTERTOP with a damp cloth. Her lab was looking particularly sparkly today. After six months of negotiating with her insurance company, her replacement gene-sequencing array was arriving today.

It had been a gruelling six months. Not only was it a personal blow, having a lifetime of her werewolf research stolen, she'd lost her livelihood. HappyGene Incorporated couldn't very well continue its work giving personal DNA analysis without the basic tools to do the job. Today was her first step to returning to a normal life.

"Hello?"

A man in a pair of grey coveralls and ball cap poked his nose in the door.

"I'm looking for Dr. Beck?"

Dr. Beck smiled and took a step forward. "That's me!"

"I've got a delivery here for you," he said, returning the smile. "Several, actually."

He pushed the door the rest of the way open. Dr. Beck could see three or four other men behind him in the hallway.

"That's odd," she said. "I was only expecting one."

The man grinned. "Must be your lucky day. Sign here, please."

She took his clipboard and scrawled her signature at the bottom, as the men began to wheel in several boxes.

"Wow, there really must be a mistake," she said. "I'm just expecting a microarray—"

"Got that one right here," said one of the men, tapping a large box. "Where do you want it?"

"Oh, um, right here," she said, motioning to the freshly scrubbed countertop.

The man wheeled the box over. He pulled a utility knife from his belt and began to unpack.

"Whoa, whoa, whoa," said Dr. Beck. "Now I know there's been a mistake. This isn't the model I ordered. This is the 56,000 series array. I ordered the 14,000."

Dr. Beck recognized the equipment immediately. She'd been admiring the 56,000 model in the catalogue for months, but she could never afford it. Even major university chemistry departments couldn't afford this type of gear without massive grants.

The first deliveryman scanned his sheet. "No mistake. Says here the 56,000 is bought and paid for."

Dr. Beck couldn't believe her ears.

"And where do you want this?" said another man across the room. He read the label on the box on his cart. "Some sort of microscope," he said. "A 'con-fo-cal' microscope? Whatever that is."

"Are you joking?" Dr. Beck said. "A confocal microscope? In *my* lab? That's worth, I mean, that's worth more than I'll make in a lifetime in this lab. There really has to be a mistake. I didn't order that."

"No mistake, ma'am," said the first man. "It's all here on the invoice. Oh, and there's one more thing." He pulled a parcel from his cart. "My instructions say to put this directly into your hands. Must be something special."

"What the—"

As the deliverymen unpacked what she could now see was hundreds of thousands of dollars of gear, Dr. Beck retreated with the smallest parcel to the quiet of her office.

She tore it open and reached in. The first item she withdrew was the hard drive to a laptop.

Her hard drive.

She reached in again and pulled out a handful of thumb drives.

Her thumb drives.

Her most precious possessions, stolen half a year ago, were sitting on her desk. Her life's research had been returned to her.

There was one more item in the parcel. She reached in and found a cellphone. It began to vibrate the moment she touched it. She swiped the screen and brought it to her ear.

"Hello?"

"Dr. Beck!" said a woman's voice. "I'm so glad to finally speak with you."

"Who is this?"

The woman ignored her question. "I trust my delivery arrived? Did I pick out the right sequencer? And I hope you like the microscope. I'm not a scientist myself, so it was a bit tricky picking out the right ones. Bit like Christmas shopping for my husband, to tell you the truth. I'm never sure what it is he wants."

"Who am I speaking with?" said Dr. Beck.

"A friend."

"A friend? Well, all of this is very nice, but it strikes me that maybe you're the same friend who was behind the ransacking of my office."

"A regrettable mistake," said the woman. "One I hope this gesture makes up for."

"What do you want?"

"It's not so much what I want," said the woman with some enjoyment. "I'm a member of an organization that simply wishes to help you to achieve what *you* want."

A beat of silence followed that statement.

"And what exactly do I want?" asked Dr. Beck.

"To find the truth about werewolves," said the woman, as if the answer were obvious. "And so, consider all of the gear in your lab a gift from Project Firefly to aid you in that quest. You'll also find your bank account is quite robust this morning. So no need to put out the HappyGene shingle any more. You can devote your life to the pursuit of truth."

Dr. Beck's heart began racing. After half a year of barely scraping by on her savings, this last bit of information was overwhelming.

"Why—"

"Because, as it turns out, we couldn't duplicate your work," said the woman. "And God knows we tried. And so, as the saying goes, if you can't beat 'em, join 'em. You can work, if not for us, alongside us. Because we have similar goals."

"What do you mean?"

"We know you can make a cure, Dr. Beck," said the woman. "That was quite an impressive bit of work. But we also know you were very close to…something else."

Dr. Beck gulped.

"Yes, we know," said the woman. "You're close to fulfilling your dream of becoming a werewolf yourself, just like your grandfather. You can turn a normal human in a werewolf."

Dr. Beck was silent.

"Let's just say: we want what you want."

ACKNOWLEDGEMENTS

I WANT TO THANK NIMBUS PUBLISHING FOR taking a chance on a story about a girl who just wants to be a duck. It is a privilege to have that iconic sailboat stamped on the spine of my books. I'm thankful for every person who works there.

I always tell school kids about how nervous I was to see the cover of my first book. Someone was taking my story and turning it into a single image? But I don't worry about it anymore. I just sit back and wait to see what Jenn Embree creates, and it's always perfect. Thank you, Jenn.

I sometimes worry I like my editor so much it might be a conflict of interest ("Oh, shucks. I'll just ACCEPT ALL CHANGES.") I love working with someone who just understands what I'm trying to say and isn't afraid to tell me when I'm wrong wrong wrong. Emily MacKinnon, you rule.

Special thanks for Dr. Karen Samis for letting me talk to her about DNA. Science!

I've never pushed my books on my kids but inevitably, as they turn ten or so, they find a copy of *Wereduck* on our shelf and start to read. "Dad," all three have said, "this is actually GOOD." My answer is always the same: "I hope so, child. I wrote it for you."

Erin, my goodness. All I want to do is play Scrabble with you. Forever and ever.

Dave Atkinson, July 2019

OTHER BOOKS IN THE WEREDUCK SERIES

Kate's family has told her that on her thirteenth birthday she'll hear the call of the moon, howl back, and become a werewolf just like them. But she doesn't want to be a werewolf. She's always felt more like a...duck.

When Kate stands near her family's cabin and hears the moon calling, it sounds like more of a "whooo?" as in "who are you?" So Kate does what she's always wanted to do. She quacks.

Kate's family has been uprooted thanks to a fellow werewolf, Marcus, selling them out to a sleazy tabloid journalist. When Kate discovers the "Cure for Werewolf," she can't help but wonder—is it really possible? Could she one day resist the call of the moon?

When John books a desperate train journey at the full moon, the ancient recipe and its arcane ingredients are put to the test.